CW01630596

UNHOLY GHOSTS

An utterly gripping cozy crime mystery

D.M. GREENWOOD

Theodora Braithwaite Murder Mysteries Book 2

JOFFE
Ostara
CLASSICS

Revised edition 2023
Joffe Books, London
www.joffebooks.com

First published in Great Britain in 1991
by Headline Publishing

This paperback edition was first published
in Great Britain in 2023

© D.M. Greenwood 1991, 2023

This book is a work of fiction. Names, characters, businesses, organizations, places and events are either the product of the author's imagination or are used fictitiously. Any resemblance to actual persons, living or dead, events or locales is entirely coincidental.
The spelling used is British English except where fidelity to the author's rendering of accent or dialect supersedes this.
The right of D.M. Greenwood to be identified as author of this work has been asserted in accordance with the Copyright, Designs and Patents Act 1988.

Cover art by Sasha Alsberg

ISBN: 978-1-80405-781-0

To J.D. who feeds me at many levels

CHAPTER ONE: EPISCOPAL TROUBLES

'It's a pity he isn't a lecher,' said the Archdeacon with regret. 'Mere drunkenness gets us nowhere.'

The Bishop sighed and gazed wearily at the opposite wall. The large Palace library, Victorian in its solid mahogany trappings, was lightly clad with the Bishop's books. He was not a reader. He felt more at home with a good filing cabinet, of which there were three, in khaki-painted metal.

'What I can't understand,' the Archdeacon went on, 'is why Dersingham put Marr in in the first place.'

'It was his turn. We're joint patrons of the living, after all. I did the last man, Clinger. It wasn't to be expected,' the Bishop said bitterly, 'that Dersingham'd consult me first.'

The Archdeacon did not, diplomatically, point out that the Bishop had not consulted Lord Dersingham when the living had been in his gift. It really wasn't worth the effort. It would be unfair to say that Archdeacon Richard Treadwell had retired on the job, but he saw that there was no further preferment likely to come his way and, to be honest, he didn't greatly regret it. And there was little point in being provocative for its own sake. He had a cottage lined up outside Cromer. Golf beckoned. He could afford, he reckoned, to be relaxed about certain sorts of problem; namely those he privately labelled intractable. He composed himself to listen as the Bishop grumbled on.

'These backwoods men will trust each other's recommendations rather than us. He got him from Warnford-the-mad who, I imagine, was delighted to get rid.'

'Sold him on without a vet's certificate, eh?' the Archdeacon snuffled through his nose. 'I suppose from Dersingham's point of view, Clinger was an unfortunate choice. He'd scarcely be considered presentable.'

The Bishop jerked his head up. 'It isn't part of the clergy's pastoral duties to know how to use finger bowls,' he said testily. 'At least Clinger had a reasonable congregation, half a dozen confirmation candidates for me and a woman running a youth club. What have we got now?'

The Archdeacon studied the file in front of him marked 'St Benet Oldfield — The Reverend Hereward Marr.'

'No confirmands this year at all,' the Archdeacon said, running his thick forefinger down the list. 'No baptisms. Three at the Eucharist I preached at last month. Seven letters of complaint including both church-wardens, one, scarcely civil I'm afraid, from the youth club lady, Mrs Totteridge, and one from a foundation governor of the church primary school.'

'I've never known a man empty a church as fast as Marr. It's quite extraordinary. A twelve-month, Michaelmas to Michaelmas. How does he do it?'

'Changes a low church tradition to a high one. Consults no one. Fails to inform either us or his church-wardens of any of his activities. Simply disappears from the parish for a week at a time. Patronises his people from the pulpit. Talks over the heads of the children in the church school. Doesn't turn up for appointments. Doesn't answer letters. Oh, it's simple when you know how.'

'How about pastoral neglect?' said the Bishop hopefully.

'Not a chance. He's excellent at a death bed. Has a sixth sense about when they're due. Always there, and if he's not sober, they're not usually up to noticing it. Hears their confession and anoints them.' The Archdeacon, a very straightforward churchman, tried without success to keep the distaste out of his tone.

'Of course it's not everyone who could stand Dersingham,' Treadwell went on. 'Clinger told me before he left that his lordship had had him in the second Sunday he was there and told him he expected him to switch on the electric fire in the private chapel ten minutes before matins. When Clinger suggested that one of his lordship's servants might like to do that, Dersingham said, what was Clinger if not just that. Clinger, apparently, didn't have the gumph to laugh.'

'Was Dersingham joking?'

'No.'

'Do you suppose Marr warms Dersingham's feet for him on Sundays?' the Bishop enquired, impelled to curiosity.

'It's a nice point. Dersingham wasn't there the Sunday I preached, so it didn't arise.'

'Would you say Dersingham is entirely sane?' The Bishop was hesitant.

'No. On the other hand he's not mad either. It's just that he's been used to having his own way for so long it doesn't occur to him there are perspectives alternative to his own.'

The Bishop nodded. 'Well, I expect you're right,' he admitted. 'I imagine Marr does know how to use a finger bowl.'

'From personal observation, his chief expertise is knowing one end of a claret bottle from the other. He asked me back for lunch after the Eucharist. I wish I hadn't accepted. I think he was nonplussed when I did but, after all, I'm usually given lunch when I've preached. We had what he called "commons" off the kitchen table. I remember hens, large grey ones, wandering in through the back door. We drank claret out of large glasses. Good stuff, actually.'

The Bishop glanced at his watch. It was digital and said 10.33. 'Dick, what are we going to do?'

The Archdeacon consulted his watch, a fob which said twenty to eleven. 'You could say a word to Dersingham. Officially, I mean, not just bumping into him in the Lords' bar.'

The Bishop winced. At heart he still felt himself to be a pastor of the sheep. He'd started off, six years ago, fresh from a large, successful Midland's Archdeaconry. He'd been on a management course from which he had returned to speak of God as 'the perfect chairman of our meetings.' 'The New Testament teaches us,' he had told a disbelieving congregation, 'that Jesus was an administrator.' It was this willingness, free from any sense of banality, to dress traditional teaching in modern cliché, which had won him his bishopric. When he'd started out, he had wanted a diocese which worked. His modest aim was a rational committee structure, sound in-service training for clergy, evangelism of the laity: the essential foundations he'd thought, of a missionary church. 'I will baptise men and women as long as there is breath in my body,' he had declared in his enthronement sermon. The splendour of the fourteenth-century fan vaulting soaring elegantly, anciently, above him had made no comment. Ironic reserve was explicit only on the face of the organist who had known three of his predecessors.

Time had told. The Bishop felt his very fabric rotted by soft living. The proud handsome county, arrogant as their pheasants, and the comfortable prosperous city had together sapped his vitality. He'd started by thinking he could do without a chauffeur. Now he knew he couldn't manage without a butler. He longed for the austerities of the mission field. He felt guilty a lot of the time. It was getting to his digestion. But he had just enough quality not to blame others for his guilt. Evangelically he strove, even if his Archdeacon had given up.

'What's up with the man? I mean, why is he so awful?'

'It can't be much fun living next door to Dersingham and having to be grateful to him for having given you a living. And I gather the marriage cracked up.'

The Bishop looked unhappy. 'Amy, isn't she called?'

'Yes. Married him about ten years ago, I believe. No children. She spends most of her time in London. The house is a tip. There's not much support in the village apart from the non-stipendiary, Deaconess Tilley, who does half-time at the primary school and a bit in the parish if she feels like it. I think too,' said the Archdeacon with untoward frankness, 'Marr feels himself to be entitled to more success in the Church than he's actually achieved. He has the manner, or perhaps the mannerisms of a bishop without actually having become one.'

The Bishop let that one go. For him there was no gap between man and manner. Or so he determinedly told himself.

'He had ten years in Italy, didn't he, and then came back here and couldn't find anything until Warnford took him in?'

The Archdeacon nodded. The Bishop reached for his diary. 'As far as I can see we can either go for Dersingham or for the man himself. I think I'd better go for Dersingham and you'd better start keeping tabs on Hereward. In the end I'll have to see him, but I want to keep that as the reserve move.'

'Just a thought,' said the Archdeacon helpfully. 'There's also Charles Julian in that part of the world.'

The Bishop nodded. 'Ah yes, and the excellent Rosalind. Could they help?'

'Bishop Julian is very experienced pastorally. A suffragan for twelve years in East Africa. I don't know if he's on terms with Dersingham. Not many are. But he might have some ideas.'

'Right,' said the Bishop crisply, glad to be making decisions. 'Friday today. You get hold of Charles Julian and see if he's got any ideas. We'll bring it up at the staff meeting on Monday and take it from there. I'd really like him out by next Michaelmas. Then it'll be my turn to appoint again.'

CHAPTER TWO: RURAL RETREATS

The goat, an experienced old white Sanaan, pushed her tether to its limits and scarcely raised her head from the thick grass round the tombstones as Mrs Yaxlee pedalled her bicycle up the gravel track to the south porch. Bright early-afternoon August sun lit the flint church of St Benet Oldfield and a cool wind from the estuary rippled the surface of St Benet Broad to the east.

'You going on all right, girl?' enquired Mrs Yaxlee who, though she did not commune with nature, was nevertheless comradely with it. Her angular Norfolk vowels seemed especially suited for goats. The nanny raised her horned and bearded head, thought for a moment and then bleated.

Mrs Yaxlee propped her machine against the outer wicket gate of the porch and placed her two armfuls of dahlias beside the door. From the pocket of her noisy plastic mac she produced a key as long as her own forearm, its turning piece in the shape of a Latin cross. She was about to insert it when she remarked the door ajar. She swept up her dahlias with an ample gesture, pushed it open, and struck downhill for the nave. There was no time for her to draw back, nor could she save herself. The pit, immediately inside the door, received her, dahlias and all.

A hundred yards to the west of the church, the long frayed green velvet curtain of the Rectory drawing room stirred in the sunny breeze of late afternoon. The tendrils of a Russian vine, which had snaked into the house through the ill-fitting window-frame, waved as though exploring a new medium. Behind the window, the putty face watched as a Moran, large and grey-speckled with red comb and wattles picked her way across the gravel carriage sweep, paused for a moment beside the bed of unpruned roses and was swallowed up in the shadows of the shrubbery. The face at the window disappeared. Inside the grand, evil smelling hall, a cassocked figure could be seen panting and swaying as it heaved a paper sack of chicken pellets from off the hall table onto the floor. The bag came down with a thud and spilt its contents over the bare oak planks.

'Damn,' said the figure effortfully. He scooped up some pellets and pushed them into an empty flower pot, keeping his thumb over the hole in the bottom. He shuffled towards the huge front door which swung open easily. The man stumbled down the shallow stone steps, rattling the pellets in the plant pot and making clucking noises.

'Amy. Amy. Come. Come. Supper,' he called and, absorbed by troubles small and great, failed to hear the cries from the church.

* * *

That same Friday evening in August, Theodora Braithwaite drove fast down the straight Roman road which was the only road into and out of Norfolk. The sun was beginning to set. Ancient oak gave place to modern pine forest on either hand. Ten miles on came heathland alive at this time of day with heather-coloured rabbits. Then huge fields of part-cut wheat, grazed by sumptuous pheasants, marked the end of the wild and the beginning of habitation and country civilisation.

The end of the journey was in sight. With every smooth gear-change she felt the recent, haunting past slip away from her. The agonised faces of the freshly bereaved or betrayed grew less insistent. She swung the car right-handed off the main road. Hedges closed in on both sides, brushing the side mirrors and sending up a cloud of small white moths into the bracken scented air. The signposts at last began to mention Oldfields in some form. Oldfield, Oldfield St Benet and Nether Oldfield. Theodora tried to remember what she knew of the geography of the place. She seemed to recall that Oldfield and Oldfield St Benet were one village with a single church, while Nether Oldfield was a bit further down the road with another church. The road began to climb gentle, sandy hills which would lead eventually to the sea.

The Julians' house lay in a hollow, a quarter of a mile from St Benet's church. It was a long, low, seventeenth-century farmhouse, a mixture of pale pink brick and dressed grey stone. No two sides of its rough square were the same. The fenestration suggested frequent changes of floor level. A brief burst of prosperity in the early eighteenth century had provided a grand pilastered door case. Originally it had, perhaps, been moated, though now the remains of Edwardian gardening prevailed. Moated Norfolk, Theodora thought, and moated house, defended against the falsity, rapacity and sheer ugliness of the metropolis. Here, then, in a temenos, a holy place, cut off from the profane, she would have ten days of solitude. It would be for her a retreat, a spiritual renewal.

Theodora swung her leather valise from the car boot into the dimly-lit entrance hall. By the light of the door open behind her, she saw the letter propped against the bowl of potpourri, addressed to The Rev'd T. Braithwaite. She read:

> *My Dear Theo,*
> *Charles and I are so sorry to miss you and most grateful to you for guarding our chattels while we gallivant round Italy. The things you need to know are:*
>
> *FOOD*
>
> *There's a fair amount in the freezer which you simply must eat up. Also two wild ducks in the larder. Should be ready Wednesday.*

Fresh food — not really obtainable locally. Yaxlee's does a little in the village, otherwise it's Lambert's in Norwich.

DRINK

Charles hopes you'll try the Médoc and tell him what you think.

CAT FOOD

For Tobias is on the dresser: one meal a day on the kitchen window-ledge (otherwise the hedgehog gets it).

We've told no one you're coming so you can hermit or not as you please though I know Laura would love to see you if you felt able. (Charles says I shouldn't write this because you'll feel bound and he says you should be utterly free from pastoral duties — though he's one to talk . . .)

Mrs Marge Yaxlee comes Tuesdays and Fridays, 9 to 1 (already paid).

Spare house and garage keys in the top right-hand drawer of Charles's desk.

Charles joins me in wishing you a perfect holiday, dearest Theo, God bless,
R.J.

PS Please water (and of course eat) the tomatoes.
PPS Yaxlee says he's got a nice young bay cob if you want to hack.

Rosalind had always acted as Bishop Charles's spokesman in things non-clerical. Theodora noticed it hadn't changed. Rosalind's generous spirit beamed from the large flowing hand and the thick paper. Mentally she returned their blessing. Dear people. What joy. Food, drink, Evening Office, a walk round the garden and an early night. Tomorrow a bathe in the cold north sea and a hack out. She checked herself. Plans. The enemy of the Holy Spirit. Better maybe, perhaps, possibly.

She seized her valise and struck out for the back of the house and the kitchen. The sheer pleasure of discovering other people's domestic arrangement stirred in her. She'd stayed here once as a child with cousins but could really recall very little. A tour of the house confirmed the impressions formed from outside. The ground floor was formal with a small, early Georgian dining room, parlour and study. The upstairs was midway between farm and cottage with a lot of oak, uneven floors and chintz.

On the whole, she thought as she grilled her lamb chop, tossed the broad beans from cullender to plate and regarded the ginger-haired Tobias who had curled up companionably on a copy of the parish magazine in the centre of the kitchen table, it's an icon of paradise: a garden I did not make, a house I'm only partly responsible for and, above all, no human contacts unless I seek them out.

It was after ten and she was closing her Office Book when she heard the car in the drive. It was coming down fast. Theodora moved to the front hall and opened the door. For a moment she was blinded by the glare of headlights before she could pick out the white mini behind them. The vehicle had slowed to a halt almost opposite the front door but on the other side of the round lawn which constituted the carriage sweep.

Theodora started down the shallow steps. 'Good evening. Can I help you?'

At her voice the car engine revved into life and the vehicle accelerated fast round the sweep. Theodora jumped back in time. The gravel crunched as the tyres bit in and the tail lights receded up the drive. Theodora stood for a moment staring with puzzlement into the dark. The half-shadowed face behind the car windscreen was unhappily familiar.

Theodora recalled its tensely held eye and mouth muscles: the face of someone perpetually on the verge of panic. She had spent the last six months learning to help many such at St Sylvester's. But this particular face she dreaded to meet again. Such an extremity of misery somehow repelled, rather than attracting pity. Theodora felt a momentary spasm of apprehension. She turned back quickly into the house, closed and bolted the door and strode across to the telephone. Then, thinking better of it, she turned to the stairs. Tobias, with his tail hooked, was ready to conduct her to her room.

'I thought I'd left that behind,' she murmured to him as she began to mount the stairs.

* * *

About midnight the wind freshened from the estuary, rustling the hawthorn in the hedgerow round the churchyard. The graveyard goat was ensconced behind the headstone of Edward George Yaxlee, born 16 August 1939, died 23 July 1988. The sound of footsteps made her raise her head and pause in her rumination. Later, there were voices and the clang of metal. Later still hands loosened her collar. But since she was comfortable and occupied she felt no need to take the advantage of her freedom. In time, however, she rose and moved off to sample the hedgerow, stretching her long, white neck to nibble delicately at the tips of the hawthorn.

CHAPTER THREE: DEACONS AND HORSES

Deaconess Tilley was as broad as she was tall. Her thick dark hair was cut in a short bob with fringe. She was admirably suited to membership of a caring profession. Competently able, and only too willing to succour those in trouble, sickness or any other worldly adversity, she was well stocked with rancour against those whom she could not count as unfortunate. With the spiritual, she was less at ease. Her flat earth common sense made her instantly acceptable to large numbers of clergy whom she in no way threatened by any daunting scholarship or ambiguity of perception. She had large legible handwriting, was good at making lists and persevering in telephone calls to the social services on behalf of the inarticulate. Apparently troubled by no drop of imagination, she was, nevertheless, a prey on occasion to night-time fears. Burglars, rapists, and mad dogs haunted her dreams. But on waking she pushed these resolutely aside and stomped out to do her good deeds.

Now, on Saturday morning, she thumped on the cottage door and at the same time leaned back from her ample waist and called up at the casement window. The blistered brown paint was peeling off both door and casement.

'Mrs Yaxlee. Can I come in, dear?'

Without waiting for an answer she laid hand to door. It did not yield to her. She was about to go round the back when the casement on the ground floor creaked open and an ample hand appeared followed by a full face, framed by thick straight grey hair, secured with a slide.

'Who is it?'

'It's me, dear. Pat Tilley at your service.'

The hand disappeared and then reappeared holding a key.

'Here, catch and come in.'

Mrs Yaxlee, by no means the eldest of the clan (there was a great aunt of eighty-seven who lived in independent squalor at Nether Oldfield) but still a senior member, sat in her parlour surrounded by the trappings of her state. Her leg, amply bound in hospital crêpe bandage, stuck out in front of her. A single toe, the big one, had fought its way to the surface to gaze at the world like a yellow ivory eye.

Deaconess Tilley was not one to shrink from such sights, but she turned her attention away from this one. The cottage parlour looked like a stage set. Rag mats, heavy oak furniture too big for the small space, a gas mantle dangerously converted to electricity with many a swathe of woven purplish flex, provided the essentials without achieving either beauty or convenience. Deaconess Tilley plumped her bag on the table and put herself between Mrs Yaxlee and the window.

'I just thought I'd look in, since I was passing, to see if you were all right.'

'Well, clearly I arn't all right,' said Mrs Yaxlee with relish. 'And I'm going to sue Parson Marr for that hole what he left open.'

Deaconess Tilley laughed heartily. 'Put your best foot forward did you?'

'You've a right to expect better of the Church than that,' said Mrs Yaxlee self-righteously. She liked a good blame and saw great possibilities in this one.

'I don't suppose Hereward dug the pit specially to catch you in, dear,' said Deaconess Tilley. She hardly knew

Hereward Marr, but since her ordination had called all priests by their Christian names on the principle of brotherhood of the clergy.

'That don't matter what he intended, do it? It's what he done what matters. Reckon that'll cost me pounds and pounds, what with the pain and the inconvenience and that.'

Deaconess Tilley did not intend to get involved in that one. 'All right for food are you, dear, or shall I pop round the shop for you?'

'The boy come early.' She indicated the huge white cut loaf on the dresser and the half empty milk bottle beside it. 'What I do want, I want my medicine what the hospital said I had to have.' She indicated the folded paper lodged against the clock on the mantelpiece.

'Righty ho,' said Deaconess Tilley. 'I'm going into Norwich this afternoon. I'll drop it in round sixish. Shall I change your library book at the same time?'

'No,' said Mrs Yaxlee stonily. She considered it an impertinence to come between a reader and her literary taste.

'I got my amusements.' She indicated the immense photograph album on the table before her.

Deaconess Tilley glanced at it with simulated interest. 'My, you were grand. In your glad rags and no mistake.'

Mrs Yaxlee considered the large sepia print on its deckle-edged mount. 'That weren't me. That were the family.'

For a moment Deaconess Tilley couldn't place 'the family'. 'Dersinghams?'

'There aren't no other round here. That's Mr Louis, that's Mr Leopold, that's Miss Vanessa, that's Miss Victoria.' Her fat finger with its yellow nail, the sister to the one poking out of the crêpe bandage under the table, followed the faces of the four young Dersinghams. Their eyes were identically glazed in male and female as they stood on either side of a seated broadclothed patriarch. The boys, about eleven and thirteen, resembled each other, a different family likeness linked the rather older girls.

'Nineteen thirty-eight. My dad were the photographer. I held the plates for him. In the rose garden.'

'That's nice,' said Deaconess Tilley perfunctorily.

'Come to a bad end,' said Mrs Yaxlee with relish.

'Really?' Deaconess Tilley looked at her watch. 'Well, I'll have to love you and leave you now, dear.'

'Nasty death, it was.'

'See you about sixish, then.'

'Killed the old Baron.'

'Be good. Don't do anything I wouldn't do.' And having exhausted her stock of phrases, Deaconess Tilley gathered her bag and left.

* * *

The cob was young and eager but uneducated. He had difficulty keeping track of all his legs. In particular he seemed to feel it was his rider's duty to support his head and neck. He leaned chummily on the bit so that after twenty minutes Theodora's arms ached with the weight.

'I think, sweetie, you're going to have to manage on your own.' Theodora allowed the rein to run through her hands and Cranmer tripped in surprise. On a loose rein, however, slowed down by Theodora's seat and guided by her legs, he began after a bit to do better. Finding he could cope, he began to swing his back and both rider and horse presently grew more comfortable.

The country was bracken-clothed dunes, the plants so tall that they came over the horse's withers in places. On one side of the bridle path ran the long low flint wall of Dersingham Park, on the other, the estuary. The estate had set its face against development of any kind and neither bungalow nor caravan blemished the coast for five miles either way. Every couple of hundred yards faded and rotting noticeboards announced that the land was private, trespassers would be prosecuted, by order of the Dersingham estate. The gates at less frequent intervals were of iron, heavily padlocked with rusty barbed wire entanglements evilly woven into the top bar. Timber rotted where it had fallen. She had heard enough from the Julians to recognise in the disrepair something of the troubles of the Dersinghams. The local big family, Rosalind had said, were as decayed as their timber.

Theodora drew rein on top of one of the dunes. The house beyond its strip of lake was clearly visible. There was a lot of it and it started early, in the fifteenth century, and ended late with Edwardian conservatories. It was apparent that there had been money at all periods except the most modern, and taste at some. The lodges and bridge were solid stone and flint classical, the stable early Victorian. Theodora's eye traced the architectural joke. The central block was originally Jacobean but had been Gothicised in the late eighteenth century. So skilful was the refacing that, at first glance, it was easy to mistake the romanticised for the original. It had the theatrical, rather gimcrack, air of many such Regency excesses. Theodora noticed the blinds were drawn in all but the central block. It was of a piece with the neglected timber, the weedy gravel and the minatory notices which guarded the bounds. The house was never shown, the garden aided no charitable cause. The parish church, older than the oldest part of the house, with its attendant Rectory, squatted a quarter of a mile away on the edge of the estate, joined to the village by a delta of ancient footpaths which successive generations of Dersinghams had been unable to close.

'Survivors, but embattled,' said Theodora to Cranmer who had got his head down and was experimentally working tufts of bracken into either side of his bit. He gave her the courtesy of a single long attentive ear. The sound of the car caught Theodora's attention before she could plot it with her eye. Then she saw it, a white toy, coming fast up the house drive before turning sharply off behind the stable block. Theodora applied her left leg and Cranmer was surprised to find he could do a very creditable turn on the forehand.

'Oh dear', said Theodora, as she gazed after the familiar vehicle.

* * *

Theodora leaned over the white rail fence which formed the fourth side of Yaxlee's yard. She watched Cranmer, loosed from his labours, wander off in an uncoordinated trot to join his friends. There was a warm sweet scent from the tidy muck heap. From far off there came the sound of a tractor. A couple of BMWs and a new Lambourne suggested the status of the clientele.

Theodora supped the hot sweet Indian tea from the thick mug and turned in answer to Henry Yaxlee's courteous question.

'They're in Italy for ten days. Tuscany, I think.'

'So this is your first visit here?'

'I came here years ago as a child with cousins from Norwich, just for the day.'

'I thought perhaps you were a relation?' Henry wasn't nosy but he liked to get things straight. He'd lived all his fifty-odd years in Oldfield and felt the duties of a host towards visitors, especially those who came with the proper recommendation.

'No. My father was a friend of Charles Julian at the university and they kept up.'

'Old friends are best. More forgiving.'

Theodora smiled at him. She found his broad fair face and calm, unemphatic manner as restful as his horses did. He reminded her of a large, slow wherry.

'You work in London then?' Henry pursued with admiring pity.

'Yes. I'm serving as a curate in a large south London parish, St Sylvester's Betterhouse.'

'You're like our Miss Tilley then, a deaconess.'

'I'm in deacon's orders, yes.'

'I can't see anything against it myself,' said Henry largely. 'Our man doesn't do a lot. At least Miss Tilley visits. Do you like the work, then?'

'Yes. Yes, I do. I like meeting different people. And if I sometimes see them at their worst, I sometimes see them at their best as well. I like,' she ended up diffidently, 'to be of use.'

'Ah,' said Henry comprehendingly, 'that would be your calling then. Like I like to bring on a good horse properly. Set him on the right path with a good education. There's no point in having a good horse flesh and spoiling it, is there?'

Theodora, too, understood this. She changed tack. 'Do you see much of your Rector's wife, Mrs Marr?'

'Amy, No, she's not been too well recently, I understand. Spends a lot of time in London . . .'

'I thought I saw her car here just now, going towards Dersingham's house.'

Henry could summon no interest in this.

'You've got some splendid beasts here,' Theodora said, reverting to a topic more likely to command his attention. 'Is it all jumpers and point-to-pointers? You don't do anything finicky like dressage.'

'We've got a couple of dressage horses at livery. Miss Vanessa keeps hers here. But mostly, yes, it's point-to-pointers and jumpers.'

'You breed?'

'Oh, yes, and deal.' Henry turned his large, open face towards her. Theodora was six foot one. Henry was just about on her level.

'Can't resist a sale. That's where the money comes from. When it does. Can't make money out of livery nowadays. Hasn't paid this century.'

'But you keep the odd hack?'

'Always glad to oblige the Bishop and Mrs Julian,' he said suavely.

'Your buildings are magnificent, in spite of livery not paying this century.'

'The boxes,' he gestured to the other two sides of the yard, 'have always been here. The school,' he indicated the other short side, 'was my grandad's. He came home from the July meeting at Newmarket in 1904 and set men on the following week. Mare called "Inspiration". I won't say we never looked back but it completed the range nicely.'

And indeed the substantial Edwardian brick and stone school made a handsome fourth side to the yard. It was clear that Henry wanted to show it to her. Theodora had no objection at all. They paced together across the black brick paving. It all looked to Theodora like a flourishing concern. Something paid, if not livery.

Henry put his shoulder to the left wing of the double door and it slid easily back. They stepped together into the school. The light flooded down from five roundels high up on the far long side, as though in a cathedral clerestory. There were no modern concessions to spectators, like a gallery, to spoil the austere sixty-by-twenty-metre oblong.

On the far long side, his grey form set off against the freshly raked dark tan of the peat floor, Theodora saw what she had clearly been brought to see. A Hanoverian stallion, with thick neck and muscular quarters, was moving as lightly as an Arab in a balanced, energetic, collected walk. As she watched, the quarters moved a fraction further underneath him and, thinking about each foot in turn, he began a cadenced and elevated pace of trot on the spot. The degree of the animal's impulsion made the movement appear to be both fast and slow at the same time. For about thirty seconds the spectacle continued. Then the rider relaxed his legs, the horse moved off into a working trot, the rider rising so much at one with the animal that he in his turn appeared to be a performing a piaffe. As the pair reached the open door, they halted perfectly square. The horse's ears, which had been slewed attentively back, swivelled in the direction of the two watchers as the rider let the rein run through his hands.

Theodora saw he was a small-bodied, long-legged boy with straight reddish-brown hair, dressed in stained fawn jodhpurs and a black pullover with holes in both elbows. He looked elated.

He glanced at Henry, 'Yes?'

'Oh yes. He's a fine fellow,' Henry allowed.

'No. Me,' the boy insisted.

'Yes, you're a fine fellow too, now and again.' Henry turned towards Theodora. 'Miss Braithwaite, Leon Securo, my head lad, for the moment.'

The boy gave a neck bow but offered neither hand nor eye to Theodora. He fiddled with the buckle of the rein and seemed undecided about his next move.

'Sponge him down and turn him out,' Henry said.

With a swift movement, the young man dismounted and brought the rein over the horse's head. As though performing a ritual, he stationed himself at the point of shoulder and walked the horse between Theodora and Henry.

'I thought you said no finicky dressage.'

'Boy's exceptional. He's only here for a year. As much to learn English as anything else. There's not much I can teach him about riding, as you see. Though he could pick up a bit on the stable management, if he'd a mind. Like most lads, he's idle. Likes the flashy stuff. Mucking out and pulling manes bores him.'

'Where's he from?'

'Italy, his dad's a customer. Takes a dozen a year off me if I can find them for him. Little Italians like large horses.'

'And the grey's yours?'

'Miss Vanessa's. But she's agreeable to having the boy do a bit of schooling.'

'Who wouldn't be?'

'Well, she's usually particular who rides Leopold, but she seems to have taken a shine to the boy. And of course she's getting on a bit herself now. Must be pushing seventy.'

'They've got huge stables at Oldfield. Why does she keep her horse here?'

'Horses. We keep her hunters as well. His lordship doesn't ride himself. Reckons it's too expensive to keep stable staff so we have the honour. And honour's about all it is. She keeps two hunters here all the year round as well as the grey and I haven't seen a penny in livery in all of five years. Since he's our landlord for best part of our grazing, we don't have much option.'

Theodora was surprised at the bitterness in his tone.

'Miss Vanessa lives with her brother?'

'Since the old Baron died.'

'I seem to remember Rosalind saying there were two sisters and two brothers.'

'The elder brother died during the war. Miss Victoria was killed over fences Festival of Britain year.' Henry's eye kindled at the memory. 'Very traditional it was. We brought her in, four of us carrying her on a wicket gate. Her back broken. A fine way to go.'

Theodora thought so too. 'She couldn't have been terribly old.'

'Thirties, I suppose. I wasn't much more than a boy myself. Can't have been much of a life. It was beginning to fail even then.'

Theodora wasn't sure she followed him.

'The estate was mortgaged up to the hilt in the thirties when farming wasn't paying. Things picked up in the forties, of course, during the war. But he was that stiff-necked, the old Baron, and Mr Louis, the present Baron, he's the same, they couldn't make it pay even when times got better. The House ate money. The gossip was they lost a fair bit in the stock market. They wouldn't try anything new. Wouldn't sell either. But sell rather than build. Must have got rid of nigh on a thousand acres all told. And mixed farming instead of taking up his hedges and going for wheat or sugar beet like the rest of them.'

Henry was launched into what was clearly his special subject, the history of modern British agriculture with special reference to East Anglia. Perhaps scenting less than total absorption from his audience, he concluded, 'Like us, if we'd have clung on to liveries when it wasn't profitable. People always will want horses but they want them in different forms at different times. You can't hang on to the past.'

'They're always beautiful,' said Theodora. 'And we can learn so much from them, if we choose to. Of course, they're also a link with the old way of life.'

'Nobility on the cheap,' said Henry.

'Cheap?'

'Without the generations of serving and commanding. And dying for both.'

'A romantic view.'

'A Norfolk view.'

Theodora considered this ambiguous attitude to the past. On the one hand Henry Yaxlee had clearly survived and prospered where the great family had not, and he'd achieved his success by breaking from the past. On the other hand, he obviously felt that the past exemplified virtues which he admired. She rather wondered what Dersingham and Yaxlee said to each other when — if — they met.

'Is Cranmer available tomorrow,' Theodora enquired, 'about the same time?'

Henry said almost apologetically, 'I think we could do you a bit better than Cranmer. Mrs Julian didn't mention how much you might have done and it's better safe than sorry . . .'

'I won't, I think, hurt anything you have.'

'I can see that,' said Henry generously.

CHAPTER FOUR: NOBILITY AND CLERGY

'You're greedy but you haven't the sense to see how to make money. Yaxlee's offering a perfectly reasonable price.'

The tweed-coated figure continued to stare at the page of the book to the left of his plate, ignoring his companion.

'We've got used to being rich and now we aren't,' she went on. The springer which had been lying buttered on the floor midway between the two slewed an eye in the direction of Vanessa Dersingham when she spoke. Since her words didn't appear to be an invitation to food, he returned his intense concentration to the man. The handsome parlour, with its lime-wood panelling reaching to the ceiling, smelt pungently of roast meat, woodsmoke and dust. 'I wonder if Leopold would have done better. If father hadn't killed him.' Vanessa Dersingham paused, waiting for a response.

Dersingham took a dark-coloured paisley handkerchief from his sleeve and wiped his lips and then his nose with it. The hands were large and bent with arthritis. He resumed poking at his meat with his fork.

His sister tried again. 'Amy came to see Hereward this morning.' The triangular face with its auburn hair and pale eyes flicked towards Louis speculatively. She sat like a small spruce viper, neatly coiled opposite him. 'I saw the car come up the drive and then turn towards the Rectory. I thought we hadn't seen the last of her.'

Still deprived of a response, she played another card. 'I thought priests weren't supposed, to divorce?'

'What would you know?' said the man suddenly. 'What would you care? An authority, are you, on the moral law?' His voice was husky with small use and his tone derisive. 'Anyway, they aren't divorced.'

'Yet.'

'Ever.'

'Why not?'

Louis Dersingham was clearly annoyed to find himself having answered his sister in the first place. 'Nothing would be served by divorce.'

'Nothing was served by marriage, by all accounts.' Her laugh was deep and pleasurable to her.

Louis pushed his plate away from him, took the chop bone and tossed it to the springer who caught it with a single sharp snap.

'Where are you going?'

'Norwich.'

'What?' she said incredulously. He might have been talking about weekending on the moon.

'Want anything got.'

'What on earth are you going to Norwich for?'

'My business, not yours.' His tone this time was pure nursery. Two siblings capping each other.

'You shouldn't be driving. Your eyesight's not good enough,' Miss Dersingham said with exasperation. 'One of these days you'll kill yourself.' She sounded as though she cared.

Her brother ignored her. 'See you,' he said jauntily, 'later.'

* * *

Louis Dersingham managed to drive into the city without seeing a single house built after 1860. No bungalow disfigured the roadside in his vision. The crop of council houses from the fifties and sixties, which formed a thick cordon round the outskirts of the city, claimed no part of his attention. Such solipsism came to him naturally, but he had applied himself to enhancing it as to an art of self-defence. During the twenty-mile drive, once he had left his own estate, he had kept his mind fixed on the goal of his errand, and what came in between went unremarked. He resented having to drive himself, but since old Yaxlee's death, it hadn't seemed worthwhile (his sister would have said, 'financially possible') to replace him.

He steered the ten-year-old Daimler under the Dersingham arch and drove straight into the cathedral close at the same speed he'd used to cover the miles from Oldfield. He pulled up in fourth gear at the foot of the balustraded stone steps which led up to the solicitor's office: Totteridge, Spruce and Hardnut, Commissioners for Oaths, said the brass plate. He took the scuffed leather document case off the seat beside him and banged the door shut with the violence of someone who had not learned that car doors do not need the same sort of treatment as those of railway carriages. The porter, whom he had swept past at the entrance to the close, hurried up, his peaked cap rattling to and fro on his small head.

'Hey! You can't park in the close without a . . .'

Dersingham did not bother to look at the man. 'My name's Dersingham,' he said, 'like the gate.' He nodded in the direction of the medieval arch through which he had just driven.

'That don't matter what your name is. You still can't park here less you've got a . . .'

Louis leaned towards him and said with enormous venom, 'You're in my way.'

Involuntarily the man dropped back, propelled by the disproportionate violence of Dersingham's manner.

'That don't matter what you're called,' he bravely persisted, 'that'll have the law . . .'

Louis, genuinely, did not hear him. His anger was real but so continuously felt that once he had given it adequate (in his own mind) expression, it ceased to modify his actions. He stamped heavily up the stone steps, through the door, along the stone-paved entrance hall. Without knocking or hesitation he entered the left-hand door, drew up a chair and, with full and accurate expectation that he was awaited, opened his document case, threw the photographs on the desk and said, 'That's the proof then. Now, I want him found.'

* * *

'Bertie moved into this totally derelict deanery just after Petertide. He found a man keeping geese in his kitchen and a woman with a typewriter in a turret.'

On the opposite side of the cathedral close from the offices of Totteridge, Spruce and Hardnut, the Bishop's summer tea for diocesan clergy, was that very same Saturday afternoon, finding its stride. If the throng was not distinguished by beauty or birth, scholarship or piety, it made up for it in sheer vigour. The noise was a low roar. Clerical wives were divided into those who wore hats on principle and those who, on principle, did not. A decade earlier their husbands would have been in sweaters or soft collars. At the enthronement of the new man, however, word had gone out: 'a man in orders is a man under orders', the Bishop was reported as saying. 'No mufti', was the translation offered by his chaplain when rung from several far-flung parts of the diocese by those wishing to know where they stood. So the majority wore clerical collars and the ones who did not knew what they were doing. The ones who wore cassocks knew what they were doing too: they were proclaiming their business as being en route to or from the clergy's very own undisputed business of marrying or burying. The only two who wore soutanes talked only to each other. The Deaconesses were identically habited in blue suits with, to a woman, clerical collars. It might have been a uniform although in fact it was not.

The Palace's ample walled garden was set like a box of sweets at the foot of the cathedral tower. Honeysuckle and lavender scented the air, espaliered coxes would, in time, delight the taste, a late flowering Variegata di Bologna crowded the eye with its opulence. Only the knot garden at the far end was bare of flowers.

There, clergy wives, listening eagerly to their husbands' superiors, would find their feet gripped by apparently supernatural growths from the infernal regions. At least one such, brought down on her ankle, had to suffer the ministrations of the Archdeacon's cheerful wife, trained, (who did not know it?) as a nurse.

Yet the conversations droned on, undiminished. 'The man's geese had carbuncles and the lady typewriter had cobwebs in her in tray so Bertie gave the hen man notice to quit and sacked the woman. After all, no one had warned him,' continued the tall fat soutane to the small fat soutane. The small fat soutane nodded sympathetically.

The refreshments were patchy. Part had been provided by the local caterers, part had come from the Palace kitchen. The word went round: stick with the Palace. Cucumber sandwiches, therefore, delicious; sausage rolls — poison, fruit scones — good, cheese ones — chalky; left-hand tea urn — strong tea, right-hand tea urn — weak. Experts in such matters to a man and woman, they soon caught on.

The Bishop and his party of senior clergy, suffragan, archdeacon, dean precentor and residentiary canons moved on oiled heels from group to group, pair to pair, solitary to isolate. Deaconess Tilley, following in the wake, patted one such on the shoulder and he spun round like a top.

'Top of the morning to you, Derek,' she said heartily. 'Long time no see'.

Her object, a Northern Irish succentor who looked, in spite of his beard, young enough to be one of his own choir boys, smiled back at her with real warmth. At least she wouldn't either bully or patronise him, his usual lot amongst the cathedral clergy, ranking as he did at the very bottom of the cathedral hierarchy.

'Hello, there.' He genuinely had a Northern Irish accent but he found himself, as many did, responding to Miss Tilley's own vivid patterns of speech by exaggerating his own. 'How's tricks in your neck of the woods?' For a moment he could not recall where on earth she was based.

'Oh, we soldier on. Though between you and me old Hereward's a bit of a liability.'

Oldfield St Benet, of course, he had it. The appalling Hereward Marr.

'On the QT, sooner or later,' said Deaconess Tilley knowingly, 'the top brass are going to have to step in.'

Derek pricked up his ears. All gossip about the failures of parochial clergy nourished him in his downtrodden state.

'Frankly, I think he may not be all there in the top storey.' She tapped her forehead graphically.

'Really?'

She didn't need prompting. 'He's taken to repairing the central heating in St Benet's himself. He dug this whacking great hole in the floor like a tiger trap and caught one of the flower rota in it. She was none too pleased.'

'Why?'

'Well, she jolly near broke her leg.'

'No. I mean why did he start repairing it himself?'

'The PCC wouldn't give him a bean towards getting it repaired and he said he'd spike their guns and do it himself.'

'Can he do that?'

Miss Tilley was no expert in parochial regulation. 'That's what the top brass will have to decide. How about getting a cuppa before the wells run dry?'

They moved towards the left-hand urn, sliding through the crowd of their superiors as smoothly as serpents in the garden.

'. . . So the red mite hen man stood outside the deanery for a fortnight with a placard: "DEAN BUTCHERS GEESE". The lady typewriter swept the cobwebs from her in tray and proved to be more of the modern world than might be expected. She unearthed her contract of employment, took the Dean to an industrial tribunal and got five hundred for unfair dismissal. No notice,' said the tall fat soutane to the small fat soutane, as Tilley and the Irishman wormed by. The Deaconess had lodged her cup against her bosom and was keeping her sword arm free for the cucumber sandwiches. Thus accoutred, she could take on all comers.

Eyeing her progress from a short distance Archdeacon Treadwell recognised his duty. He was a thick man. Thick hair, thick eyebrows, nose, lips, shoulders and tailoring. The question was sometimes asked whether he was also thick-witted. Years and heredity within the Anglican Church (his father had been a colonial bishop) had so formed his manners and speech that it was sometimes thought so. Certainly he was incapable of being indiscreet, losing his temper or being unkind. He moved now towards Miss Tilley and her acolyte, smiling.

'Miss Tilley, Pat, how are things in your neck of the woods?' He at least had no difficulty in recalling the parish in which she worked. 'I hear Father Marr has taken to digging pits for the unwary.'

The Deaconess was not in the least surprised that the Archdeacon knew of Mrs Yaxlee's accident. The speed of light was slower than the intelligence of the clerical network in matters of gossip. The disaffected Vicar's warden had been on the phone to the Archdeacon's secretary by five-thirty on Friday evening.

'We soldier on, Dick.' The Succentor heard with fascination the familiarity which, stemming from a naivety as colossal as Miss Tilley's could hardly be resented but for which he nevertheless found himself blushing. Yet the Archdeacon, he noticed with admiration, appeared unperturbed.

'*Entre nous*,' said Miss Tilley ineffably, 'old Hereward's a bit of a case. Bit of a problem at times. I mean, frankly, does he know anything about the inner workings of central heating?'

'You reckon?' said the Archdeacon, essaying the demotic in response to Miss Tilley.

'Wanted to put one over his wardens, I reckon. What with the increased quota we're short of bobbins.'

'How about a donation from the patron?'

'Mean as church mice', said Miss Tilley drily.

'I seem to remember,' said the Succentor, feeling he ought to figure somewhere in the conversation, 'some very grand tombs in St Benet. Money sometime obviously.'

'Sixteen ninety and eighteen ten', said the Archdeacon. 'Also a crusader couple. Good lettering at all periods. However, I think I'd better take a peep at the excavations. When, I wonder, would be a good moment?'

'I'm doing matins tomorrow at St Nicks, Nether Oldfield. Hereward's doing the eight o'clock at St Benet. So you pays your money and takes your choice.'

'I'd like to hear you preach, as well as taking a look at the excavations,' he said dutifully. 'Fourth after trinity: "passing through things temporal that we lose not things eternal", I seem to remember.'

'I'm saying a word on boot sales,' said Miss Tilley complacently.

A lesser man than the Archdeacon would have made a mental note to avoid this rash abandonment of the riches offered by the Prayer Book collect in favour of a misshapen modernity. 'Really, to what end?'

'Can't spill the beans. Trot along and you'll find out.'

The Succentor smothered a snigger and moved politely off towards his former refuge. '. . . So, then, the lady typewriter set up a stationery shop in the High Street with, it is supposed, the contents of the Dean's stationery cupboard. She had a particularly fine line in funeral cards,' he overheard the tall fat soutane say to the small fat soutane as he wandered by. The party rumbled on.

Two minutes later, in the far corner by the hollyhocks, the Bishop's chaplain, with an unobtrusiveness which suggested considerable social aplomb and boded well for his making the bench himself in due course, levered the Bishop out from a tight knot of clerical wives.

'An accident,' he murmured. 'Fatal, I'm afraid. The phone's waiting.'

* * *

Theodora wiped her hands on the damp grass and lay down again beneath the currant bushes. The point about picking currants was that there was absolutely no temptation to eat the crop. The Julians subscribed to the idea that one grew and was grateful for whatever the country best produced. Years abroad had made them grateful for yams, bananas, cocoa beans and rice. Now, in their Norfolk retirement, they doubtless said their grace for currants, white, red and black. Theodora knew them all to be bitter, seedy and indigestible. But she too had a keen sense of making the best of whatever was given. It just seemed a pity that Norfolk should have no more appetising soft fruit. Had they, she wondered, ever tried raspberries?

Lying on her back and deftly working upwards through the small mottle-leaved bushes, she allowed her mind to drift towards the recent past. The white car with its half glimpsed driver's familiar face accelerating up the Julians' drive haunted her. And what had that car been doing again this morning in the Dersinghams' drive? She had resolved to put all such problems behind her. She hadn't realised that it might be here in Norfolk that the origin of the problem could lie.

When she had packed her bag at Betterhouse Vicarage on Friday morning, she had thought only of the holiday she had so badly needed. The kind Julians had offered their house and on an impulse she'd accepted, relieved only to be free from the demands of the parish. For the last six months, since her return from Africa, the work had been heavy and continuous. Aware that there was no accepted path for women in deacons' orders in the Church of England, she had nevertheless looked around for a curacy which would put her in possession of solid parish experience. St Sylvester's

Betterhouse, on the south bank of the Thames, upstream from Lambeth, fitted her bill. The parish was large, poor and ethnically diverse. Sikhs jostled Greeks in the street market; Turks rivalled Chinese in the restaurant trade. There was a vigorous life, both commercial and family, carried on in the basements of large Victorian terraces. She had taken an immediate liking to the Vicar, the Reverend Geoffrey Brighouse, an ex-naval officer who had matters well-organised and from whom, she had quickly realised, she could learn a lot. He ran the parish church, a nineteenth-century barn of a place, on liberal catholic lines, avoiding any extremity of churchmanship. He had shown her round the parish with such an enthusiasm for its social and ethnic diversity that she had warmed to him and, when offered the curacy, accepted. Finally, there had been the additional attraction of the Foundation of St Sylvester's Betterhouse.

The Foundation was housed in a large Edwardian villa next door to the church. It had a permanent warden, the Reverend Doctor Gilbert Racy, and a fluctuating staff of what Theodora privately dubbed para-clerics. It acted as a retreat house and training centre for people attached to the Society of Saint Sylvester but, under Racy's leadership, it had made a name for itself specialising in an area of the church's work which Theodora thought was undervalued. The healing ministry earned no one a bishopric, and the healing of minds was as neglected and underfunded in the church as it was in the National Health Service. Nevertheless, Theodora knew she had skills which could be valuable there. She knew how to listen with active goodwill, while at the same time her sceptical and meditative temperament saved her from any impulse to change or manipulate clients. She knew by instinct that healing change can never be imposed on people from outside. It was an attitude which, she suspected, Racy rather valued. She had been invited to 'do' a couple of mornings a week for Racy. It would, he had informed her at their first meeting, be mostly a matter of watching and listening for the moment. Later, if she showed any skill in the area she had better go and train. It was in the course of that initial watching and listening that she had come across Amy.

Clients were known by their first names only. Without access to case notes and forbidden as part of her training to ask direct questions of either Father Racy or Amy herself, Theodora had at first found it hard to place her either in terms of her problem or socially. Theodora judged her to be in her early forties, though the thin face and fair, wispy hair made her look younger. She dressed in an unvarying uniform of black ski pants and pink mohair pullover which became grubbier as the weeks passed. In the daily group sessions Amy had said little, preferring to fix her eyes on the blank wall above the heads of her fellows . . . Occasionally she would allow her gaze to drop on to one of the other patients with a look which Theodora could only interpret as startled amazement. Occasionally too she would simply sit crouched on the sofa and weep silently, her hands pressed to her cheeks.

Theodora had followed her brief and for three months she had watched and listened. At the end of that time she had learned that Amy was married to an Anglican priest and felt herself trapped and manipulated in a relationship in which she was the inferior partner. Amy had gone into some detail as to how her husband had effected that state of affairs but beyond that, prevented partly by her inexperience, partly by her natural reserve and partly, indeed, by the barrier which Amy's misery put up, Theodora had not penetrated. Amy had left the Foundation a week ago. It was not etiquette to enquire where clients went, so Theodora had asked no questions. Had she known where the husband's parish was, Theodora asked herself? She seemed to remember that Gilbert had mentioned East Anglia. She had not, however, until last night, supposed that her husband might have a living near the Julians. She wondered whether Amy had been looking for the Julians or for her when she drove down the drive? And why was she looking? Theodora was torn between curiosity and irritation. She wanted a holiday. She wanted a rest from the likes of Amy. On the other hand she had set her hand to the plough. She needed to learn as much as she could about this area of mental disturbance.

Theodora caught herself up. She must stop worrying. What was intended she would know in due course, and whatever she was required to do would be made clear. She gave herself the pleasure of recalling Henry Yaxlee and his calm sea-like presence. There came, too, the image of the thin, nervous boy rider, so far from his native heath, totally absorbed in producing delicate movement from the heavy horse.

'Good afternoon', said the Archdeacon. The voice broke Theodora's reverie.

She unfolded herself carefully from the prickly bushes and rose to her feet. Her tattered shirt and ancient denims in no way detracted from her tall decorum as she gazed down upon the squat clerical figure. She smiled with genuine pleasure.

'I'm afraid I may not be what you are looking for. The Julians are on holiday. I'm keeping house,' she said.

'Ah, yes. I see.' It had been a long day. The Archdeacon's disappointment was courteously hidden.

'I'm so sorry you've had a vain journey. Would you care for tea? Or indeed, by now, sherry?'

'Either would really be most welcome.'

Theodora gently steered him back to the house and set him in a deckchair on the south-facing terrace. He looked with relief at the pale yellow liquid frosting in the generous Julian glass.

'May I know to whom I have the pleasure . . . ?'

'Theodora Braithwaite.'

'Braithwaite. Now, would you by any chance be in deacon's orders?'

'You may have known my . . .'

'Indeed I do. I have the happiest memories. Richard Treadwell.'

'How do you do? The Archdeacon then?'

'For my sins. I hope your father is well?'

'He died last year.'

'My dear girl! I am so very sorry. How could I not have known?' The Archdeacon accused himself at many levels, not the least professional. He read *The Times, Church and Financial,* and the *Independent.* How could he have missed it? Norfolk, of course, was off the map — but all the same . . . However, the goal posts having been established, it did make it all much easier.

'Have you had a chance to sample the local fare yet?'

'I only got here last night. I thought I might try Nether Oldfield for a matins tomorrow or, I believe there's an eight o'clock at St Benet.'

The Archdeacon thought of Deaconess Tilley's promise of boot sales. He gazed at Theodora's unemphatic handsomeness and felt an irrational wish to protect the cumbersome Miss Tilley from Theodora's unspoken, he could not doubt, criticism. He tried to recall what he knew of Nicholas Braithwaite's only child. He seemed to remember something about Cheltenham, Oxford and Nairobi. Not, definitely not, at all events to be let loose on Miss Tilley.

'Have you considered the cathedral by any chance? The music is excellent and the Dean is doing matins.'

'Is something wrong with the local menu?'

It was a measure of the strains of the day, or perhaps of the relief at finding the sympathetic Theodora, that the Archdeacon was precipitated into something close to indiscretion.

'The local man, Hereward Marr. I'm afraid he met with an accident last night. In fact he was killed.'

There was the slightest pause in Theodora's breathing.

'How very unfortunate. Poor man. How did it happen?'

'He may, it's possible that . . .' the Archdeacon had not had time to formulate the appropriate phrases to describe events. 'He was found in St Benet's with his neck broken. He'd dug a pit. The central heating,' he concluded lamely.

Theodora was able to form no clear picture of the accident. 'You mean he fell into a pit which he had himself dug which was connected with the building's central heating system?' She tried to keep the incredulity out of her tone.

The Archdeacon nodded unhappily. It was untidy. It was undignified. It was un-Anglican. It would undoubtedly lead to a lot of administrative activity. It was all he most hated.

'When?'

'The police seem to think it happened sometime after midnight last night.'

Theodora thought of Amy and the car in the drive. 'When was he found?' she enquired.

'Mrs Totteridge, a parishioner, came to check her goat about lunchtime, went into the church and found him.'

'So you're on your way to see Mrs Marr?'

'Partly that, though I gather the police haven't been able to trace her whereabouts as yet. I really came to have a word with Charles Julian. I was hoping he might feel able to support me in breaking the news to the Dersinghams.'

Theodora said slowly, 'I think I may have known Mrs Marr.'

'You were a friend?'

'Not exactly. I'm serving a curacy in South London at St Sylvester's Betterhouse. There's a foundation attached. Perhaps you know it?

'The Foundation of St Sylvester? Gilbert Racy?'

Theodora nodded. 'They run one or two groups for people in distress. I think I may have come across Mrs Marr, Amy, in one of them.'

'She was seeking help? To what end?' The Archdeacon looked more than interested.

'I expect you know, the foundation gives people a chance to relax physically and mentally. We offer some therapies to help them regain confidence in themselves so they can express and release some of those tensions which are causing them to behave irrationally.'

'Was Amy Marr irrational?'

Theodora hesitated. The Archdeacon appreciated the point. 'I'm not gossiping,' he said gently. 'We know, that is, the Bishop knows, that there are, were, problems. We shall be seeking to help.'

Theodora blushed. She had not meant to imply that the Archdeacon was idly curious.

'The problem, as it often is, was her relations with her husband.'

The Archdeacon waited.

'She indicated that she found him overbearing. Indeed at times violent.'

'Was she telling the truth?'

'Mrs Marr was far from well herself. She'd been under medical care.'

'She was deluded or exaggerating?'

'She was clearly deeply unhappy and frightened.'

'Were her fears rational?'

'I'm not an expert in that field.'

'But you felt they might be?'

'I could see no reason why she should have invented them.'

The Archdeacon sighed. 'I fear we have to blame ourselves in such matters. We simply do not have the structures or the resources to give proper pastoral care to clergy wives. Or indeed to those clergy who themselves fall by the wayside. We expect everyone to be preternaturally fit all the time. I'm sure that in itself creates strain.'

'Since however Mr Marr is dead . . .'

The Archdeacon cheered up. 'Yes. Possibly it's all for the best. Though, of course there'll have to be an inquest. My next task must be to tell the Dersinghams. We're joint patrons of the living. Marr was Dersingham's appointment. It will be the Bishop's turn this time round.'

He manifested such reluctance to get up that Theodora felt constrained to recharge his glass.

'I've not met the Dersinghams,' she said, to give him time.

'A difficult family,' said the Archdeacon gratefully. 'I don't think it does anyone any good to have been on the same patch of ground for five hundred years. My grandfather, who kept a small number of sheep in the West Riding, used to talk about strains breeding themselves out. In the end families like the Dersinghams seem to be held upright by the social system without actually having anything very much to contribute to it. That's what seems to have happened with the Dersinghams.'

Theodora nodded to encourage him.

'The mother of the present Baron was drowned when her dinghy capsized in St Benet Broad just before the war. 1937. Her husband, the old Baron, as the locals call him, died about ten years later. His heir preceded and indeed, I think, precipitated, his death.'

Theodora raised an eyebrow.

'The boy hanged himself. The elder sister, Victoria . . .'

'Killed over fences.'

'You've heard?

'Stable gossip.'

'She was a fine rider, I believe, but reckless.'

'Who's the heir?'

'There isn't one either to the title or the land. That's part of the trouble. Louis has never married. The surviving sister, Vanessa, likewise. The entail from the grandfather was on the eldest son. They've always married near kin and there is just no cousinage. I remember hearing Hardnut — their solicitor — saying that Dersingham had spent a fortune trying to trace someone to leave the place to.'

'To no effect?'

'Apparently.'

'What would happen to it? Couldn't Dersingham leave it to someone he designated or adopted, something like that?'

'Well, yes, but Dersingham is desperate for a Dersingham to inherit. His whole effort is towards nothing being changed. He'd not leave it to someone who would turn it over. And even if Dersingham *did* want to adopt an heir, who would want to be adopted by Dersingham? And frankly, who'd want the place anyway, in its present state? It would cost a fortune to make the house watertight. The farms all need investment. The timber went in the twenties and the shooting with it. Really Dersingham has his name and not very much else in the way of either sense or property.'

The Archdeacon realised he had been carried away, cleared his throat and gulped the last of the sherry. 'Well, I suppose . . .'

Theodora thought rapidly. She liked Treadwell. She was, she had to admit, curious about the Dersinghams. She recalled the desperation on Amy's face behind the car wheel last night. Amy was in her pastoral care, even if she was on holiday. If help was needed Theodora could not, she knew, in all conscience, refuse it.

'I know I'm no substitute for either of the Julians,' she said at last, her tone carefully diffident, 'but if you would like me to come along? If Mrs Marr had by any chance returned, I might be of use.'

The Archdeacon looked immeasurably relieved. 'My dear girl, it would be so kind of you, but I hardly like to trouble you.'

'I'll go and change,' she said.

* * *

The manservant who let them in looked too young and too tall for his black coat. Floppy, fair hair of identical length all round, brushed his collar behind and just missed his pale wide-set eyes in front.

The Archdeacon nodded kindly to him, 'Evening, Yaxlee. How's your grandmother's leg?'

'That's going on all right, sir, though she don't like to admit it. She was cursing poor old Reverend Marr up hill and down dale but I don't reckon even grandma wanted him dead,' said the lad with relish. He was indeed young.

The hall in which the manservant greeted them was theatrically lit from the Regency gothic windows of stained glass which threw the early evening sun in coloured patterns on to the black and white marbled floor. The draught from the door raised the edge of the ancient carpet in a moment's suspension. Young Yaxlee stamped on it, as he paced before them, as though quelling an insurrection. Theodora glanced up at the gallery above them and the blue and white fan tracery which arched over it.

She and the Archdeacon followed Yaxlee into what had once been the library. Now the white painted bookcases which reached to the ceiling were filled only on the first two shelves with incongruous modern volumes with used-looking dust-covers. Delicate chairs with frayed green silk upholstery were placed round the walls. The only other furniture was an enormous wooden tapestry frame with a small chair in front of it, set up in the recess of the tiny bay window at the far end of the room. In the chair crouched the figure of Vanessa Dersingham, stitching a tapestry.

Above her on the wall hung a portrait in the manner of Laszlo showing a woman in her forties. She wore a purple dress and was seated on one of the green silk upholstered chairs. The bronze hair round the triangular face was cut in a short bob so that it curled to razor sharp points like horns on either side of her ears. Her eyes, of indeterminate colour, set far apart, protruded slightly. She was looking out of a window towards a view of the park.

Vanessa Dersingham paused between each stitch. She was seated far enough away from the frame for her every stitch to seem like a considered attack. Her bronze hair, with no trace of grey, was cut in a short bob so that it curled to razor sharp points like horns on either side of her ears. Her eyes, of indeterminate colour, were set far apart and protruded slightly. She wore a dark purple dress. Theodora wondered quite what point Miss Dersingham was making at so resembling presumably her mother's style of dressing. They waited, but Miss Dersingham did not turn or greet her callers.

'He's escaped you then?' she said without preamble.

'Escaped?' The Archdeacon said cautiously.

'Weren't you pursuing Hereward?'

'Not exactly'.

'Well, if you weren't, you should have been. I would have.'

'What had you in mind to pursue him for?'

'What you should want to pursue him for might be different from what I would pursue him for.'

The Archdeacon didn't feel he wanted to do any pursuing.

'I hadn't realised the news had already reached you. Otherwise . . .'

'Otherwise you would have spared yourself the journey. There's nothing that happens on the estate which I don't know about. Did you enjoy your ride?' She swung round to Theodora.

'I did. The horse didn't.'

'One of Henry's untutored geldings.'

'Your country's absolutely unspoilt.'

'Louis' one virtue. And an expensive one.' Whichever way the conversation turned, Theodora reflected, it seemed Miss Dersingham was determined to bring them up against topics which could not be elaborated on. Her aggressive conduct in conversation mirrored her methods in embroidery.

The Archdeacon had had enough. 'I'm sorry to have intruded . . .'

'Upon our grief.' The tone was ironic.

'I wondered, however, if you knew where Mrs Marr was now. The police haven't been able to trace her and we shall have to arrange an inquest — and of course the funeral, which she will naturally need to be concerned with.'

'Naturally.'

The Archdeacon waited. When pushed he could be just as awkward as Miss Dersingham.

'I don't know where Amy is. Have you tried Benet Broad?'

The Archdeacon looked baffled. 'I can't see . . .'

'I understand her car was found in the Broad a couple of hours ago . . .'

The Archdeacon disliked everything that was being said, and showed it. 'Was she in it?'

'The police didn't mention it. Perhaps she bailed out before the fall.'

'What time did Mrs Marr leave the Rectory this morning?' enquired Theodora innocently.

Miss Dersingham looked with hostility at her tapestry. 'I really haven't the remotest idea.' Miss Dersingham's deep cultivated voice was in a dying fall.

Theodora noticed Miss Dersingham had not denied that Amy had visited the Rectory. It was likely that, just as Theodora had seen the car from the bridal path, Miss Dersingham could have seen it from the House.

They had not been asked to sit down and indeed there was nowhere for them to do so. The spindly chairs against the walls were not up to it.

'I think we should not trouble you further,' said the Archdeacon with finality. 'Should you see Mrs Marr return . . .'

'You will be the next person to know of it, be assured, Archdeacon.'

Theodora and Treadwell retraced their steps. As they reached the front door, it flew open in their faces. The evening breeze once more did its trick with the carpet and the tall arthritic figure of Louis Dersingham limped in. The Archdeacon and Theodora stepped back to give him passage. The Archdeacon opened his mouth to greet him. Dersingham looked to neither left nor right but strode across the hall and began to mount the uncarpeted wooden staircase. Three steps from the top he turned his head and shouted with immense violence over his left shoulder into the dark recess beside the stairwell.

'Yaxlee!'

Without waiting to see if the young servant materialised, Theodora and Treadwell stepped through the open door and into the freedom of the outside world. The Archdeacon, to Theodora's amusement, mopped his brow. It was a perfectly appropriate action, but she'd never seen anyone do it before as a gesture of relief after social effort.

'Not a novice ride,' she said sympathetically.

'They're all difficult. I'm never sure whether their vile manners are the result of too much breeding or too little.'

'It can't be too little, can it? Didn't you say five hundred years on the same patch?'

'Stuff's run out.'

'No point, I suppose, in checking the Rectory? Just in case Amy Marr has returned?'

They swung off down the weedy gravel, skirting the grand, derelict stables and following the drive until it became a track and the land began to rise. They smelt the salt of the estuary. The church tower loomed up from its promontory and beside it Theodora saw the solid block of the seventeenth-century Rectory. Tall lime trees hedged its roughly scythed lawn. There was utter stillness. The red bricks of the house looked grey in the late light. Its various creepers, wistaria, magnolia grandiflora and Russian vine had been checked at the level of the first floor. They gazed at it together, united by beauty and silence.

'Practically the only good thing which can be said about the patronage system,' said the Archdeacon, 'is that it prevents dioceses selling off or pulling down at least some few of their beautiful buildings.'

'I thought all archdeacons wanted clergy to live in modern bungalows based on designs derived from the local constabulary?'

'True, so we do. We have to balance the books but we can still allow ourselves to regret it.'

Theodora watched a large, grey speckled hen parade slowly across the sweep, pause, raise an enquiring eye to the front door and pace on into the shrubbery.

'Should we feed it, her or perhaps them?'

Duty was deeply bred into the Archdeacon. They mounted the shallow steps of the house. Theodora raised the knocker and let it fall. As it did so the door swung open. The silence of the hall received them. Theodora glanced down at the floor. A dark stain was discernible running intermittently from the door to the bottom of the stairs. They both gazed at it. Then Theodora bent down and ran her finger along it.

'Water, I think.'

They searched the house together, neither wishing to admit the unease (amounting in Theodora's case to dread) which the unexpected and unexplained sight of the water prompted. What, Theodora wondered, would they find next?

At least the house's symmetrical plan made it easy to encompass. As they moved from one high-ceilinged panelled room to the next, signs of disorder and decay met them at each open door. It was impossible to escape an impression of lives deeply disturbed and unhappy. There was little furniture anywhere. The dining room had a table but no chairs. Plants, unwatered, had died painfully in the drawing room. There were plates — not always empty — wedged in odd places. The library had nothing on the shelves but the floor was littered with volumes open and lying face down. A number of glasses of various kinds sprouted from between them like some bizarre flower bed. Of the four bedrooms, two had beds in them and only one of them had bed-clothes on it. Neither the bathroom nor the kitchen had been cleaned recently. The door to the servants' quarters in the attics had been nailed up. There was no human presence discoverable anywhere.

'Ought we to lock up, drop the latch?'

The Archdeacon nodded. The stench of the frowsty rooms as much as the picture of the misery of its inhabitants left him pale. Theodora took a couple of handfuls of the chicken pellets from the split bag in the hall and broadcast them over the gravel. The Archdeacon swung the door to.

'The water?' said Treadwell experimentally.

'Might have come from Mrs Marr. Or on the other hand, I'm sure you noticed, Lord Dersingham's trousers were dripping wet.'

CHAPTER FIVE: DOCTORS AND FISHERMEN

Doctor Laura Maingay changed her sandals for driving shoes, pulled on a pair of string-backed driving gloves and wound a silk square over springy brindled hair. She shut her eyes and turned the ignition key, pressing it slightly to the left. If she kept her eyes open the car very often failed to start. She had been a scientist long enough to know this is, in practice, how the world works. The ten-year-old Morris Minor rolled like a small cherubic tank down the short drive of her bungalow in Nether Oldfield. There was little traffic on the Norwich city ring road at this time on a Sunday morning.

At the mortuary door she saw a police sergeant talking to Dennis, the duty nurse. Police nowadays were either very young or very old. This one was old. Dennis was saying with the petulance of an apprentice relying on his master's authority, 'The sergeant says, could they have the report by half-eleven. I told him. No way, I said.'

'Morning, Sergeant', said Dr Maingay kindly. 'What's the rush, then?'

'I expect it's because he's a clergyman, or was, miss.' Doctor Maingay was fifty if she was a day but was widely known to be unmarried. 'Can't have a clergymen being dead on the Sabbath, can we, Sergeant?' This piece of whimsy baffled the sergeant so he pressed on, 'The inspector said, if you could let him know the cause and time of death, he'd be very grateful. His number's up . . .'

'. . . on the board,' Doctor Maingay responded.

At eleven forty-five, Laura Maingay switched off her cassette Dictaphone for the last time and ran it back to the beginning. 'Lungs . . . contusions . . . vertebrae.' As she listened to the playback she gazed at the naked corpse. The heavy Roman-emperor head with thinnish iron-grey hair brushed forward, the nose, broad and fleshy, and the mouth fallen in for lack of teeth, was not a comely picture. The rime of silver stubble round the heavy chin and above the mouth suggested the beard was still growing. Devoid of animation, lacking the divine spirit of life, if he had not been a priest she would have thought the expression petulant, the top lip folded over the lower one in resentment and self-pity. What, she wondered, had brought him to this ungainly death?

She stopped the machine, took off her gloves and overalls, did a lot of washing and pushed through the swing doors into the empty Sabbath calm of the shabby corridor.

'Dennis, lovie, can you type this out now and let me have a copy? And switch the phone through to my office.'

Seated at her capacious desk and stirring a cup of herb tea, Laura began her conversation with Inspector Spruce. Spruce said at intervals, 'Are you sure, doctor?' And Laura would answer, 'Nothing is certain in science, but nevertheless it looked as though . . .'

She liked Spruce, a colleague of some years now. When she'd first qualified in forensic medicine he'd been a young sergeant. They'd come up together in the crime world she reflected, and she was sorry that her findings were clearly causing him trouble.

'What you're saying,' Spruce said, 'is that he was dead before he got into the pit.'

'Quite right, Inspector.'

'Oh hell,' said Spruce. 'Nobody's going to be pleased about this. Could he have had a fall or tripped or something?'

'That's not likely is it? I hate to say this but I do rather think from the bruising that someone did it to him.' Laura paused, the better to relish the effect of her words, then added, 'There ought to be a special word for a priest-slayer, don't you think?'

Spruce's immediate response was inaudible. 'Any idea of when?' he asked finally.

'Not long before midnight and not long after either,' Dr Maingay said authoritatively. 'More precise than that I cannot be.'

'Fine. Fine. Many thanks for your help. I'll be in touch. You're not going away or anything?'

'Rest assured, I'm at your disposal,' Laura replied pleasantly.

By noon Spruce had rung the *Eastern Daily Press* about a press conference, and his Superintendent about a case conference. The Superintendent had rung the Bishop. The Bishop had rung the Archdeaconry. Mrs Treadwell had rung Deaconess Tilley who had returned from matins at Nether Oldfield with the Archdeacon in tow. The Archdeacon had said, 'Oh dear' a number of times and driven off, refusing Miss Tilley's offer of a bite of hot-pot.

Theodora, freshly returned from the cathedral's matins and a tramp round Norwich, ate her Sunday luncheon about half-past two, on the terrace, with Charles's Médoc and Blomfield's *Essay Towards a Topographical History of the County of Norfolk* from Charles's library to hand. Tobias sat on the *Independent* and helped her with the pheasant pâté When the phone rang, faintly audible through the open window, she was in two minds about answering it. But it went on.

'Theo, dearie?'

'Gilbert?'

'The very same. How are you?'

The familiar stress on the first word in the sentence took her at once into the stuffy room in south London. The Victorian drawing room which had become the office of St Sylvester's Betterhouse Retreat Centre came vividly before her. She could picture Gilbert Racy's actorly, emaciated profile, and his tall, cassocked figure. She could see the Italian bondieuserie and complete edition of Migne's *Patrologia Latina*, round one wall and a comprehensive collection of Christian psychology, mostly emanating from American or Dutch publishers, round the other.

'I'm supposed to be on holiday. How did you find me?'

'I know you are. It's too bad. Your Archdeacon called me.'

The devil he did, thought Theodora with admiration. What right had that harmless-looking father-figure to be so noticing? And so quick off the mark.

'Mrs Marr,' said Gilbert Racy suavely.

'Yes,' said Theodora resignedly.

'Do you know where she is?'

'Do I know? No, of course not. Don't you?'

'You sound just like your Archdeacon.'

As a member of a monkish order, Gilbert took little account of parochial and diocesan systems. For him, archdeacons did not count. All the same, his detachment irritated Theodora.

'He's not my Archdeacon. And I don't know where Amy Marr is. I take it that Mr Treadwell wants her about her husband's funeral?'

'Well, actually I think the police want her about her husband's death first.'

'Is that what Mr Treadwell said?'

'More or less.'

'When did Mr Treadwell ring you?'

'About twenty minutes ago.'

'Why are you ringing me?' Theodora couldn't help feeling, as she had felt before when dealing with Gilbert, that he was being disingenuous.

'I thought you might need to know.'

Now he was definitely manipulating. What *did* he want, she wondered. 'Gilbert, what is all this? Are you just stirring it, or is there something I should be doing?' Guilt, easily aroused, stirred within her as she guessed he intended it should. Damn Gilbert.

'Theo, my dear girl, your country sojourn has made you hoydenish. Naturally I'm curious. I'd also like to help Amy if she's in need. I gather the police think she killed her husband and then drowned herself.'

Theodora wondered if she'd heard Gilbert aright. 'What?'

'Drowned herself.'

'No, I mean, how do you mean *killed* her husband?'

'The Archdeacon says the post-mortem showed his neck was broken. They also say Amy's car was found yesterday afternoon dumped in a pond near the church.'

'Broad,' said Theodora abstractedly.

'Well, I expect they'll be dragging it by now.'

'If Amy Marr's dead in the Broad, I can't see there's much I can do. Though how she could possibly have killed her husband, I can't think.' Theodora realised this was rather a lame attempt on her part to steer clear of what was increasingly looking like a nasty piece of wreckage.

There was a pause, then Gilbert's high clear voice came again. 'I think she may not be in the pond . . . Broad.'

Theodora felt she'd had enough surprises. 'What?'

'I gather he died between midnight and one, Friday night. I think Amy phoned me about seven last night.' Was it satisfaction she detected in Gilbert's tone? Almost as though he relished the piling-up of horrors.

'How do you mean, "you think"? Don't you know whether Amy phoned you or not?'

'One can never be entirely sure of anything in this world, can we, Theo?'

'Gilbert, don't be tiresome. What did she say last night?'

'She was naturally rather overwrought. She mentioned a box.'

'Box?'

'You don't know anything about a box, Theo?' The voice was precise and insistent, almost authoritative. Theo remembered it well from groups where Gilbert interrogated, requiring truthfulness. It was a tone compelling difficulties to be faced and not evaded.

'No, Gilbert, I don't know anything about a box of Amy's. Are you saying she left some of her trappings at Betterhouse when she was with us? I imagine there might be a box there. Where was Amy ringing from when she called you?'

'She didn't, I think, mention that,' Gilbert sounded detached, as though it would have been ill-mannered of him to enquire.

'Have you told the police?'

'Really, Theo.' Gilbert sounded genuinely shocked.

Theodora understood this to mean no. If Gilbert Racy took little account of ecclesiastical structures, his attitude to secular ones was solipsistic. It would not, at one level, matter to him if one of his patients was a murderer. The greater the sin, the more glorious the struggle would be his attitude. He treated all human relations of any depth on a par with the confessional. This made him very successful, since utterly trusted, with certain sorts of client. At other times it seemed near to irresponsible madness.

Theodora wondered which it was in this case. It was on the tip of her tongue to tell him that she thought she'd seen Amy on Friday night. Instead, however, she said, 'You do realise, Gilbert, that there'll be an inquest in which the likely verdict will be murder?'

He blithely ignored her. 'If you come across Amy, I think it would be best if you put her in touch with me rather than trying anything on your own.'

'If I come across Amy Marr, surely I ought to put her in touch with the police or possibly the Bishop?' Theodora felt the vanity of attempting to propose some measure of common sense on Gilbert's waywardness even as she spoke.

'I shouldn't do that, sweetie,' he said. 'They aren't very likely to be able to help her, are they? And the souls of the living are more important than those of the dead, who, as you know, are in the hand of God.'

'But Gilbert . . .' She felt sudden panic, as though he'd left her comfortless, holding a problem. The problem of finding Amy.

'You've got my number, haven't you? Bye, Theo, God bless.'

The line went abruptly dead. Theodora replaced the mouthpiece and the telephone shrilled again as though it had been waiting for her to release its ring. With deep foreboding she lifted the receiver.

'Miss Braithwaite? Richard Treadwell here. I wondered if you could possibly spare us a moment of your time tomorrow? I hate to interrupt your holiday but it would really be most helpful if you could.'

They agreed to meet at ten-thirty the following day at the Archdeaconry. Beneath Treadwell's courtesy it was not difficult to detect his anxiety. He was about to ring off when, on an impulse, Theodora said, 'I wonder if I might visit St Benet's? I mean, could I get in?'

She didn't want to. She hated the idea of it, but she was spurred by the thought of Amy and by the phone call from Gilbert Racy. Where was Amy now? Where had she gone after appearing in the Julians' drive on Friday night? The same place she'd gone after driving up the Dersingham's drive on Saturday morning? Might there be some clue to her whereabouts in the church, she wondered? And, most awful of all, was Amy a murderess?

The Archdeacon hesitated. Finally he said, 'I think the police have the porch key but I seem to remember there's a key to the vestry door in the north transept. It's a Yale lock, and I'm sure Bishop Julian will have a spare of it. I'll let the police know you'd like to enter.'

* * *

George Yaxlee took the contents of the back pocket and laid them on the mantelshelf. He spread the trousers carefully on the large deal table, put the towel with which he'd been drying the luncheon dishes carefully on top of the faded tweed, smoothed it into place and began to poke out the creases with an old iron. There was no sound from the rest of the house. The cold tap dripped into the stone sink at long, regular intervals. The kitchen door stood open revealing a strip of bumpy grass and yellow, sandy gravel wide enough for a coach and four to turn in between the House and the stable block.

George let his mind wander over the House. He'd known it all his seventeen years. Both his mother and father had worked there. His only certain memory of his mother was of her looking out of the same kitchen window and calling to him as he played on the grass. He must have been about five. When his father had died twelve months ago and his grandmother had made it clear she wasn't going to give him a home, he'd wondered what would happen to him. He'd left the local school as early as his birthday would allow and hadn't really done anything for the following year except watch his father die.

The day after his father's funeral, his grandmother, Mrs Yaxlee, told him to go and ask his lordship for a job. 'That'll mean you won't have to move out of the coach house. That way you won't be beholden to no one.' Except, presumably, to his lordship. 'And put a clean shirt on and polish up them shoes before you ask him,' had been her only subsequent worldly advice. He hadn't the heart to say he didn't want to be his lordship's servant or, indeed, anyone's servant. He wouldn't mind going for a labourer, though there weren't that many jobs; nor would he have minded going down to his uncle Henry Yaxlee's yard to help out with the horses. But he didn't like to go against his grandmother who, in her grim fashion, had been kind to his dad at the last.

If he felt resentment that the Yaxlee family network had failed him, he wasn't of a nature to allow this to embitter him unduly. Thus it was that his greatest hurdle to date had been asking his lordship for a job. He'd never spoken directly to the man in all his seventeen years. Though his father who, in his time, had been coachman, groom, mechanic, chauffeur and handyman, had talked a lot about Dersingham, George could only rarely remember his father actually addressing his lordship. Relations between his father and Lord Dersingham had been carried on, as it were, in reported speech: what his lordship said, did, wanted; what Miss Vanessa said, did, and wanted; these were staples of the Yaxlee family conversation. Indeed, such conversations among the estate workers were not just gossip but an acknowledgement that all social relations stemmed from that source, the Dersingham family. George knew very well there was not a household in Oldfield, Nether Oldfield or Oldfield St Benet where that was not the case. Of course people talked of other things too. Crops, animals, money, football, marriage sometimes, love rarely. If George's schooling had done its job he'd have known his ancestors speaking just so. But in the end it all came back to 'the family'.

Nor did such concern arise out of snobbery. No one envied or imitated the family. No affection was felt for them, for they were consistently rebarbative. Nevertheless, by far the greater part of the emotional energy and imagination of five hundred people was rooted in the Dersingham family. They might no longer be the biggest landowners: more people now worked off the estate than on it. Economic ties might be beginning to weaken (they didn't have tuppence to rub together, did they?) but the influence was not exhausted. The architecture of three villages was theirs. Apart from their own House and the alms-houses in Nether Oldfield, their arms were on three pubs, their monuments in two churches, the one surviving primary school was on their land. The tithe barns, the Rectory, the toll bridges no longer controlled daily life, but they still punctuated the landscape. And that landscape, too, had had its contours formed by the family. They had drained marshes, diverted roads, uprooted hedges, planted trees and felled them, preserved game and in due season, hunted it. As in landscape, so in social relations. However eccentric and reclusive the family members, they had taken their seats in the Lords, been County Councillors,

Parochial Councillors, Justices of the Peace, chairmen of this, patrons of that. When they entered shops, people yielded their place to them and were silent or civil. Social ties might be beginning to weaken but ancient attitudes and expectations could still — just — be relied upon. And in his turn, Lord Dersingham would never have thought of recruiting one of his servants from anywhere except from among those born on his own land.

Finding, therefore, the opportunity, marshalling the words with which to approach his lordship, had been something of a rite of passage for George. He chose the time carefully, lurked and caught Dersingham as he was coming from the stable yard after having driven himself out. This was shrewd on George's part since it meant that Dersingham had done something which George's father had been wont to do and which, in fact, Dersingham hated having to do for himself. George had pushed his hair out of his eyes, cleared his clogged throat and said, 'Please, sir. Would you consider letting me do my dad's job for you?'

Louis looked at the boy whom he had clearly never seen in his life. 'Who?'

'Ted Yaxlee, sir.' Dersingham continued to look vacant. 'He was your dad's — your lordship's, the old Baron's. And he worked for you till he got sick. He was the one that just died, sir, last Monday. He used to drive for you.'

'Ah. You drive?'

George hesitated. It was clear to him that if he said he could, his lordship would take him. But George was afflicted with a truthful nature. He could in fact drive quite well. He'd driven his lordship's car under his father's instruction, but he had no licence.

'Just about to take my test, sir. I know a bit about engines. My dad taught me. And I can mend things, on the whole,' said the honest boy.

'Live near?'

'In my dad's quarters, sir, at the moment. South side of the stable block.'

Self-interest gleamed in Dersingham's eye, rendering him almost articulate. 'What about the House? Serve food, clean up, valeting, answer the door a bit?'

'I think I could serve and clean and so on. I'm not much of a hand cooking.'

'No need. Got a woman. Two women in fact.'

'I could start tomorrow, sir.'

'Month's trial. Fiver a week. All found.'

That was the last time George had felt any affection or gratitude to old Dersingham. So here he was six months later valeting his clothes on a hot Sunday afternoon when any normal youth would be outside.

George whipped the trousers off the table and placed them on a hanger which he attached to a wooden creel. Though he was the descendant of a family who had done this sort of task for generation after generation, George nevertheless made it look as though he were acting. His long thin fingers at the end of the long adolescent wrists highlighted the movements. It was as though the dullness of the tasks, the strenuous but commonplace duties of his life could only be borne if they were dramatized.

It was, therefore, with exaggerated haste that he undid his black tie, pulled the white shirt over his head, substituted a red T-shirt and a pair of old Norfolk drab cords that he'd salvaged from his father's wardrobe. He glanced at the clock over the door. Ten to three. He was off till seven. Sunday's lunch was cold, supper hot. George served both but didn't cook. Mrs Marjorie Yaxlee, cousin on his father's side, would be in to do the cooking round six. He took a last look round the kitchen, caught up his flask and pack, carefully dislodged his rod from the top of the deal press and doubled out of the House. When he was fifty yards down the path he remembered the trousers still on the creel. He slowed down and almost turned back. Then he ran on. 'Let the pop-eyed brute get his own clobber if he needs it,' he muttered rebelliously under his breath.

* * *

St Benet Broad was older than Oldfield and its settlements. Dug originally, before the Romans came, for peat, by the thirteenth century the diggings had extended perilously near to the estuary. The great flood tides of Spring 1402 had swept over the low-lying marshes of the estuary and forced a passage to join the Broad with the sea. The tide had receded, the land silted again, but the plant life remembered the salt inundation: oddities and rarities of flora attracted the scholarly and delighted even the uninformed. Today a four-mile-long expanse of shallow, brackish water, scarcely suitable for any vessel except the wild fowler's punt, reflected the immense Norfolk sky. Long brown fingers of reed stretched out into the saucer of khaki water.

The Broad lay a mile outside the perimeter wall of Dersingham Park to the east of the church. Beside it, crouched on the one bit of sand which allowed space for casting, George gave his full attention to his float. He had an interested audience of mallard, water-hen and the solitary grebe. He heard the sucking sound of Wellington boots and the rustle of parted reeds but did not look up.

'You started without me.'

'I 'arn't got much time. Come over the other side. You're in the way there.'

Leon sucked his way carefully round his host's person and joined him in gazing at the red plastic blob.

'It is called?'

'Eh? Oh, a float.'

'Float.'

'Right.'

'And what will you take by your float?'

Leon was acquiring fluency and a strong Norfolk accent. The finished effect was attractive.

'Well there are pike.' Then, to forestall the inevitable question he added, 'Big fellow with long nose. Fierce. A right terror. Eats up all the little ones, cocky ruff and such like.'

George felt no call to admit that the tackle he was using could in no wise cope with a pike. The stuffed one in the 'Lord Dersingham' bar measured three feet. He dreamed of it and of himself catching it; imagining it lunging and threshing as he played it and tussled to land it. They settled down companionably. The sun moved round, the shadows of the reeds on the opaque water grew longer. George raised himself, propped his line against a bundle of reeds and reached for his flask and pack.

'I have been sent chocolate from my mother. My cousin also has sent cake,' said Leon.

They shared George's ham and pickle rolls and Leon's dry vanilla-tasting cake and chocolate. The flask tea alone Leon jibbed at. Only then did Leon approach the subject closest to his heart.

'Tell me again of your grandfather the rider.'

'Coachman. But of course he did ride.' George remembered his father speaking of *his* father, to whose place he had succeeded. His grandfather's picture lay in his grandma's album, two from the end, showing his grandfather wearing his lordship's livery, in which he'd driven the old Baron to the coronation of King George VI in 1937. They'd driven from Oldfield to London with four dark bays. His dad had told his grandad's story with a sort of ironic pride. If the family were going to take on the outside world, they'd do it in eccentric style, his father had implied. It had taken them four days to cover the hundred-odd miles and they'd commanded attention from Larling to Epping. They took a farrier with them, not trusting to strangers en route. 'The family came back by train, though,' his father had concluded. 'Your grandad used to say it were a fine drive back with no one telling him what to do.'

'What d'you want to know?' said George.

'Tell me how he drove four horses with coach to London.'

'I told you all I know about it.'

'And the horses. They were only for coaches or they could do to ride as well?'

'Oh, they went under saddle as well. I don't think they had the money even then for separate coach and riding horses.'

'They went in red coats?'

'No. Gentlemen's coachmen dressed very quietly in those days. They had long brown coats and brown bowler hats and boots. The only fancy bit was the buttons. They were in silver with the family's arms on them. My grandma's still got my grandad's stuff somewhere.'

George stopped. He realised how much he longed to wear that splendid sober regalia and take up a whip to drive a team of four horses. He could almost feel the immense cluster of leather reins running through his hands. It would be a sensuous pleasure as great as landing a pike.

'Can we see them?'

'What?'

'Can we see the big brown coats with the silver buttons of your grandfather?'

George considered. He quite understood Leon's interest. He himself would have gone anywhere to see a set of tack of strange cut or history. What gave him pause was not lack of sympathy for the enterprise but the appalling difficulty of handling his grandmother in relation to Leon. He could think of no form of words, no common interest which could provide a path down which they could all three go abreast.

'What could we say?'

'Say?'

'To grandma? We'd need a reason, like.'

'Say, I like the story.'

'Story. What story?'

'The story of ancient times.'

'History.'

'Sì.'

George thought there might be something in this. His grandmother liked to talk of past times too. But would she like to do it with a stranger and one so strange as Leon who came, not just from ten miles off, but a thousand? He looked at his friend's neat copper head and wide-set eyes.

'Here,' he said kindly, 'You cast this time.'

Leon laid his hands to the rod and George noticed how they were bigger, stronger, altogether more mature and experienced than the rest of him. Riders' hands. They wound in the line and re-baited from the mass of wriggling brown gentles in a tin. Leon cast with creditable fluency, well beyond the encircling reeds. Both were so absorbed in their activities that when the float went down, they did not at first respond. Then George realised what was happening. With great self-restraint, he did not grab the rod from his friend's hand. Instead he whispered hoarsely, 'Gently, gently. Let her out then draw her back.'

Gently Leon let her out and then drew her back. The line taughtened then stuck. He tried again. This time the line first tautened and then twanged loose. Leon wound the reel rapidly. Both boys kept their eyes on the end of the line. With a sucking noise, its end broke the surface. Dangling from the hook came a length of rope and a piece of leather larger than a dog collar, large enough, indeed, to have fitted a goat.

'That's not a pike,' said Leon. 'Shall we throw it back?'

George wiped the collar with its short length of tether on his cords. 'You never know,' he said. 'Might come in handy. Pity about the hook. Try again.'

* * *

Theodora, leaning against the balustrade which crowned the tower of St Benet's church, glimpsed George's red T-shirt in the distance. From the top of the tower she could survey the whole of the surrounding country. On her high perch, she had the familiar feeling of exhilaration and apprehension. The warm, soft-seeming lead beneath her feet and the sharp-knapped flint and stone under her hand only partially secured her against the deep fear of falling. Looking down the tower, she could see, twenty feet below her, the church roof and the back of the necks of the gargoyles roaring noiselessly over the marsh.

Theodora had found the spare vestry key, neatly labelled, in the top right-hand drawer of Charles Julian's desk. The policeman, who had materialised out of the hedgerow when she approached the churchyard, had had her name written in his notebook. The Archdeacon had done his stuff. She had climbed the seventy-nine steps to the top of the tower and rested there beside the cupola. To the east was the Broad, to the south, the estuary, to the west the Rectory. Beyond that there was the House with the village at its gates.

Henry Yaxlee's stable lay west of the House, at the far end of the village, where it was hidden by a belt of tall chestnuts. Beyond this again, a few hundred yards down the road, lay the right-hand turning to the Julian's. The bridle path, which Theodora and Cranmer had traversed yesterday morning, could clearly be seen meandering from the back of the stable between the estuary and the wall of Dersingham Park. It passed the back entrance of the Rectory, skirted the churchyard and divided in two, one leg going to the Broad, the other turning left to the main road. Along it, Theodora could just make out a lone rider heading back to the stable. There were no sounds except the cry of the gulls. The remoteness of the place, its un-changingness and lack of any trace of the modern world awed her. How long, she wondered, could this precious solitude hold out?

This, then, Theodora reflected, was the parish, the most ancient division of civil society in Britain. Hereward Marr had had charge of the spiritual wellbeing, the cure of souls, of three villages. How had he managed? Had he daily prayed for the church and the world? Had he taught the young, visited the old and comforted the afflicted? Had he sought to bring all sorts and conditions of men into God's saving presence? By all accounts, or at least by his wife's, that had not been his first concern. Theodora had passed none of that on to the Archdeacon, and he had himself offered no judgement. Had he known or not? Perhaps his motto was — speak no ill of the dead — especially dead priests. Somewhere in the church below her, forty-eight hours previously, Hereward had met his death. Who, she wondered, had hated him enough to break his neck?

Theodora had not wanted to become involved. She wasn't sure that she was equipped to help, but the habit of clerical obedience was part of her inheritance. If Gilbert thought it was part of her duty to track down Amy or help her in any way, then she would do so. She had little choice. And besides, the vision of Amy's drawn and frightened face continued to haunt her. For a few moments more Theodora continued to enjoy the spectacle of gulls and swallows swooping and idling on the warm air. Then she descended into the cool, light church. She knelt to pray — for the soul of God's servant Hereward, his wife and all who worshipped there. After that, she turned to the task for which she had come. She inspected each part of the building minutely. She wasn't entirely sure what she was looking for but she remembered what Amy had said about her husband's church in one of the group sessions at St Sylvester's. She hadn't mentioned where it was but she had spoken of it with love. She had mentioned how she tended it. Clearly she had found solace in its silence and calm, silvery light. Perhaps, she thought, Amy might have left something here. Made some sort of mark by which she could be remembered.

After half an hour she had to admit defeat. There was nothing out of order or especially remarkable in that quiet place. Finally Theodora came to rest in the Dersingham chapel which formed the south transept looking towards the altar at right angles.

The chapel had something of the calm, attentive atmosphere of a drawing room just vacated by its owners, it was splendidly furnished with funerary monuments of all periods. A pair of Jacobean Dersinghams, husband and wife in about half life-size, kneeling side by side on a plinth, looked stolidly into eternity. Their seven children, carved in high relief in diminishing size according to age, clustered round their feet like rabbits. Wall tablets assured the reader of the integrity of the blood line. Patrilineal descent and property rights were the strong ropes of the family. Aberration, if it occurred, was not recorded, and the female line took second place. Property reigned.

Theodora moved softly round the walls. Two veiled female figures leaned in exaggerated mourning over an urn in the Grecian taste of the 1810s. Whatever the Dersinghams had skimped on, it was not the accoutrements of death. Round the walls were four hatchments vividly painted with red shield and gold 'V' of the Dersingham arms, starting out from the black background. One of these seemed faintly familiar. Then Theodora remembered the tapestry which she had seen Vanessa Dersingham stitching yesterday evening when she and the Archdeacon had made their unnecessary visit. And yet, Theodora reflected, the hatchment did not quite fit her memory of what she had seen. Surely Miss Dersingham's tapestry had shown the arms in a lozenge? An oddity.

Theodora looked for the more recent memorials. The first of the current family to die had, presumably, been the old Baron in 1947. A bad time for lettering but the old Baron had known what he wanted and the lettering was excellent: plain Roman capitals. Below him was his daughter, Victoria, obit 1951. No mention of the interesting cause of death. She looked for the other, older brother whom Henry had said had died during the war, Leonard was it? No Leopold, whom the Archdeacon had said hanged himself. Perhaps the church wouldn't let him, a suicide, be buried with his ancestors. Perhaps he had been banished outside. But no, charity had prevailed. There was a small bronze plaque with decent lettering low down on the north wall. 'To the memory of Leopold Thomas Rice Dersingham who departed this life 12 July 1942 in the 18th year of his life. RIP.'

Theodora made ready to depart. She had found nothing to enlighten her about either Amy or Marr, only the powerful presence of dead Dersinghams. How had Hereward Marr, a rackety priest, come to know this rackety family, she wondered. But there was no clue here to the secrets of the living, only the trapping of ornate death. She moved towards the back of the chapel, skirting the low table of the third Lord Dersingham and his lady lying stiffly on their backs, he in his crusader armour, she in her simple pleated dress, her hands finely sculptured and pressed together in prayer. Theodora stopped, bent and looked closer. So Amy had left her mark after all. She felt a momentary triumph and something approaching relief, as if Amy had at last consented to communicate with the world. And of course, that communication, that trust, to whomsoever offered, must not be refused or betrayed. Of that Theodora was certain. Swiftly she made her way out through the south door. Suspended from a length of string hung over a chair placed beside the small pit was a piece of card. The notice said 'Danger, Keep Out.'

* * *

Leon, returning rather later than he had given anyone to understand, thought it politic to take the path through the far paddock and enter the stable yard via the muck heap. He swung himself nimbly over the fence and was disconcerted to come face to face with Henry Yaxlee, walking purposefully from the direction of the school. His employer swung round, pivoting on his heel like a soldier. For so solid and unemotional a man he might have been angry, or perhaps only in a hurry. Either way, Leon was aware that Yaxlee was exerting his considerable presence. Yaxlee looked him up and down.

'What happened to the livery feeds you were supposed to sort before you went off?'

Leon didn't feel his English was quite up to this.

'We were engaged at the fishing, *signore*. Then we caught a collar.'

'What?'

'We fished up a collar from the Broad?'

Henry stared at him. 'Look, Leon,' he said finally, almost casually, 'I can't run a stable on idle, incompetent, unreliable labour. If you're going to stay out your time here, you'll have to pull your weight. You understand?'

Not all the adjectives were known to Leon, but the drift was clear.

'*Si, signore*, I am so very sorry.'

'Get those feeds mixed and taken round now. Then rub Wellington down. He's been sweating.'

Leon didn't have time over the next hour to wonder what the energetic, highly competent and reliable Wellington had been doing to make him sweat.

* * *

George, returning to the house rather earlier than he might have expected, put his head under the cold tap and let the delicious water course over him. Then he shook his head like a dog and, spluttering a bit, pushed open the kitchen door. His aunt, Marjerie, was already at work, and the smell of roasting meat came from the range.

'Hello, my duck. His lordship's been calling for you.'

His lordship had called, indeed bellowed, so often over the last six months that George had come to expect little else. But Sunday afternoon was reckoned to be his off time. 'What'd he want, then?'

'Something about a pair of trousers.'

'They're on the creel.' George nodded toward the quaint apparatus suspended over the table. 'Or were. Did he take them?'

'No. They wasn't on the creel.' She flicked the flour expertly over the board and cut the pie shape.

'Must have been. I put 'em there before I went out. They can't have walked. No one'd want 'em. They were that old.'

'In a right old sweat he was,' said Mrs Yaxlee tranquilly.

CHAPTER SIX: POLICEMEN AND BISHOPS

Inspector Spruce placed his notebook on the polished mahogany table and waited. Archdeacon Treadwell leaned back in his bentwood chair and pressed the tips of his fingers together. As an Archdeacon should, Theodora thought, as she drafted a neat set of interlocking triangles on the sheet of foolscap thoughtfully provided by her host.

Then Theodora surveyed the Archdeacon's study. It had the basic reference texts of an Archdeacon and a fair amount of theology which dated the Archdeacon's interest in that subject to thirty years previously. There was a single filing cabinet, but in all other respects the room could have been inhabited by his father, the colonial Bishop whose portrait hung over the marble mantelshelf. Edwardian solidity had been achieved even if not exactly aimed at. Theodora wondered whether it was a room which could cope with the demands of the modern world.

The silence was strained. After an age, the doorbell rang. There was a murmur of voices below and, moments later, the study door was opened by Mrs Treadwell.

'The Bishop', she said with an air of subdued triumph, as though she had produced him against all odds.

The Archdeacon rose. Theodora rose. The Inspector rose. There was a scraping of chairs, a rustle of papers, a subdued clearing of throats. The thought passed through Theodora's mind that it was almost impossible for a Bishop to enter a room other than dramatically.

'Prevent us, O Lord we beseech thee this day with thy most gracious favour . . .' The Bishop prayed rapidly. He then did the introductions for Spruce's benefit. 'Mr Treadwell, I think you know. Miss Braithwaite,' he gestured towards Theodora, 'we have asked to join us. She has, I understand, some knowledge of Mrs Marr which she's kindly consented to put at our disposal.'

Spruce nodded to each without smiling. Theodora wondered for a moment how he would place her. She knew that as a Deacon she was still an uncommon enough phenomenon in the Church to evoke curiosity. She had, therefore, dressed to escape notice in a dark linen suit and silk shirt; she had judged it, however, to be an occasion for a clerical collar, lest the Bishop should need reminding.

'Well now, Inspector, would you like to put us in the picture?' The Bishop smiled encouragingly at Spruce in a kindly attempt to put the man at his ease.

Inspector Spruce leaned forward over his notebook and fixed his eye on each member of the party in turn. His rather careful tailoring suggested an accountant rather than a policeman. Only the thin leather belt in place of braces implied his life might be an active one. There was nothing thuggish about him but he looked like a gymnast. He looked, too, as though he might be quite hard to surprise or impress.

'I'll start with the facts as far as we know them at the moment.' Theodora noticed he had a slight Norfolk accent and no trace of nervousness or pomposity. He knew what he was about.

'On Saturday the twenty-fourth of August last at 1.15 p.m., Constable Yallop of the Norfolk Constabulary received a telephone call from Mrs Veronica Totteridge of Glebe Cottage, Oldfield St Benet. Mrs Totteridge asserted that when she went to check her goat in St Benet churchyard at 1 p.m., she had found the goat wandering loose without a collar and the door of the church open. On entering the church, she found the Reverend Hereward Marr, Rector of this parish, face downwards in the pit dug just inside the door of the south porch. She turned him over and concluded that he was dead.'

Theodora reflected that it had been really rather brave of Mrs Totteridge to turn him over. The pit was about a metre and a half deep. She would have needed to have lain on the floor beside it and leaned into it. Clearly a woman with good nerves. Had she been prompted by curiosity or the instincts of the good Samaritan, Theodora wondered.

The Inspector was pressing on. 'Constable Yallop responded to the call in person. He concluded that there had been an accident and the body was removed to the Norfolk and Norwich casualty department. The duty doctor suspected foul play and the Norfolk CID were informed at 8 p.m. Owing to the shortage of medical staff, the post-mortem was not carried out until the following morning. The verdict of that post-mortem was that Reverend Marr had been killed at about midnight on Friday. His neck was broken.'

Inspector Spruce paused. Privately, he hoped the clergy were unfamiliar enough with this sort of thing not to ask too many questions about the incompetence of all concerned. Half the force had been at the match, of course, although that was hardly an excuse. Two of the police surgeons had been on holiday and the third, Doctor Maingay, who did a locum for her father's old practice when needed, had not been available until Sunday morning.

'On that same Saturday,' Spruce went on, 'at 3.54 p.m., Constable Yallop returned from patrol along the St Benet Oldfield — Nether Oldfield road, travelling east. He noticed the fencing round the gate leading to the Benet Broad Lane to have been recently broken. He followed the tracks of a car driven apparently at speed to the edge of the reed bed. He saw the top of the car projecting above the water. The car, a white mini with a sun roof, was later identified by Albert Yaxlee, landlord of the Dersingham Arms, as belonging to

Mrs Amy Marr, wife of the deceased Rector. PC Yallop waded out and attempted to open the nearside door. When he failed to this, he attempted to enter through the sun roof. When he couldn't manage that either, he radioed for assistance. The car was raised at 4.40 p.m.'

Poor old Yallop, Spruce thought, had had quite a day of it after twenty-five entirely uneventful — and promotionless — years in the force. He went on. 'There was no one in the car and cattle had churned the ground so much that we could not with certainty detect footprints in the vicinity of the car's entry into the water. There is no trace of Mrs Marr and an alert, including radio appeals, has produced no evidence of her whereabouts.' There was silence.

The Inspector concluded, 'The questions we have to ask, therefore, and which we hope you may be able to help us shed some light on are, one, who was motivated to kill Hereward Marr; two, what precisely might have provoked them to do it; three, who drove the mini into the Broad and four, where is Mrs Marr at this moment?'

There was another silence. Theodora could see the minds of her clerical superiors weighing up their own list of priorities which, she guessed, might not be quite the same as the Inspector's. Their concerns, in order of urgency, were likely to be, one, how could they save the church from scandal and, two, how could they keep the police and the press from asking awkward questions? The task of discovering the truth or even of helping Amy would come some way after those considerations. The Bishop and the Archdeacon were old and wily but not too well-informed; Spruce, on the other hand, looked to her like an intelligent adversary. But he would be hindered unless he knew the methods and presuppositions of the Church and its clergy. Perhaps, though, he knew that he needed help. Perhaps that was why they were all here.

Her own feelings about the situation were, she concluded, ambivalent. Of course the church should not be exposed to gossip and contumely. But, on the whole, she supposed, she felt considerable sympathy with Gilbert's attitude that the Church's first duty was to Amy. The dead would have to bury the dead but the unhappy living might still be helped by goodwill. She sat back to see how each party would cope.

The Archdeacon opened the batting, clearly intent on feeling his way with caution. 'I wonder, Inspector, if we might ask you one or two questions to get a clear picture, as it were?'

Spruce nodded his assent. Was he, Theodora wondered, going to let out the line in order the better to haul it in later.

'Was anything found on Hereward's body?' asked the Archdeacon.

'Wallet with five pounds and nothing else at all. No keys.

'Was anything found in the car?'

'There was no luggage or bags of any kind. Maps, a torch, a rug.' Inspector Spruce continued. 'Our enquiries suggest that the car entered the water at about 3.30 on the same day. The landlord of the Dersingham Arms saw it driven past at about 3.20 p.m. It may have been driven around a bit before it entered the water. We can't know. We've calculated the time from how deeply it had settled in the mud. We've had no other reported sighting of it before it entered the Broad. There were no keys in the ignition.'

'City were playing at home,' commented the Archdeacon. 'First match of the season. Very popular. The coach would leave the Dersingham Arms at about one p.m. The village would be deserted of men and boys between two p.m. and six.'

'Correct.'

'Where did the car come from?'

'Miss Dersingham was able to tell us that Mrs Marr's car came past Dersingham House on its way to the Rectory at about 11.30 a.m. on Saturday morning. She was not able to say when it left.'

'Who was driving when it went past the pub?'

'The landlord wasn't sure. It went past very quickly.'

There was a pause. So much, Theodora thought, for the scene-setting. Now for the main action. She glanced at the Bishop. He was gazing judiciously at his finger nails with the air of a man content to leave the opening moves to his subordinate. She looked towards the Archdeacon and recognised the signs of someone about to take the plunge.

He took the bull by the horns. 'Are you saying, Inspector,' the Archdeacon asked, 'that Mr Marr was murdered?'

The Inspector nodded. 'Mr Marr was certainly killed by someone in the sense that his neck was broken and the doctor doesn't think it could have been accidental. I may say that I have great confidence in Doctor Maingay's judgement in such matters. She doesn't think, for example, that the bruising is compatible with his having had a fall. She's more inclined to think that his neck was broken by someone wrenching his head back with considerable force.'

'Wouldn't that be quite difficult to do?'

'It depends. If the assailant knew what he or she was doing, if the victim was either surprised or trusted him or her, it wouldn't be impossible. One fact is pertinent here. The stomach contents and blood tests indicate Mr Marr had taken a fair amount of drink immediately prior to his death on Friday night.'

'Fair amount?'

'The stomach contents were consistent with,' said the Inspector detachedly, 'say a couple of bottles of claret.'

Marr wouldn't have turned a hair on that, thought Theodora, but she said nothing.

'If his neck was broken before being put into the pit, was he killed elsewhere or in the church?' The Archdeacon liked to get a sequential narrative. He was old-fashioned in such matters.

'It looks as though he was killed in the south porch of the church. There's no sign of a struggle in the church but the facial bruising is consistent with his being forced against the wicket door. There are also blood and hair traces there. A possible scenario is that he had turned to leave the church when he was attacked from behind.'

There was a creaking of chairs and crossing of legs at such plain speaking. 'Have you any notion who might have killed him, Inspector?' said the Bishop, clearly feeling that, if matters were getting down to fundamentals, it was time he played a part.

'As yet,' said the Inspector imperturbably, 'we're only at the beginning of our enquiries. However, for the purpose of our meeting here this morning, we are discounting tramps and casual thieves since his wallet wasn't stolen. Nor do we have any reports of escaped psychopaths or violent addicts of any sort in that part of the county. Though, of course, these may come to light in due course.'

Theodora found herself intrigued by Spruce's attitude. It was perfectly respectful, but suggested he found the clergy slow to take a point. But she could not work out what the point was that Spruce thought obvious but which the clergy — herself included — hadn't grasped.

'Forgive me, Inspector,' the Bishop was almost diffident, slightly regretful, 'But how can we help you? On the face of it, it looks like a purely police problem.'

'To catch a murderer we need a motive,' Spruce said bleakly. 'We thought you might have one for us.'

So that was the point Spruce thought the clergy ought to have grasped.

Theodora watched the senior clergy failing to respond. She began to admire Spruce. He was tough and poised. He knew when to confront and when to allow evasion.

Then the Archdeacon said, 'Inspector, before you go any further, is it, in your opinion, possible for Mrs Marr to have killed her husband?'

'I'm sure you know, sir, that women do not, on the whole, break men's necks. But it depends how much they want to. It would also depend on how much knowledge any woman had. The doctor's report suggests that the fifth cervical vertebra was broken. That would be a good one to break if you wanted a quick death. And, as I'm sure you know' — the Inspector's judicious glance swept his audience — 'we can sometimes do in passion, say in passionate hatred, what we couldn't do ordinarily. If Mrs Marr knew a bit of human anatomy, for example, if she'd had a medical training or been a PE teacher something like that, she'd have a better chance of being competent, by which I mean lethal. You don't, I suppose, happen to know whether she fulfils either of those categories?'

Theodora rehearsed the facts about Amy's past life which had emerged during her time at Betterhouse. She realised she simply did not know whether Amy had that sort of specialist skill. Would Gilbert have known? If he had, he hadn't mentioned it to her.

In the meantime the Bishop reflected. 'I must have met Mrs Marr at some point.' He turned to Mr Treadwell for help.

'I think you met her when they first came into the diocese at Hereward's induction.'

'Of course. I remember now, a slight, fair, unobtrusive woman. Rather pretty. Looked as though she might well make a good Vicar's wife.'

'When would that have been?'

'Twelve months last Michaelmas,' said the Archdeacon smartly.

'September to September.' The Inspector clearly knew his church year, Theodora reflected, or was it the law sittings? 'So, by this September they would have been here not quite two years.' He turned back to the Bishop. 'It would help us a lot to know as much as possible about both Mrs Marr and the Rector. Their not being local people, we're naturally in the dark.'

The Bishop and the Archdeacon nodded intelligently. 'Any help we can give,' said the Bishop heartily.

Theodora distrusted their feigned openness. They had had plenty of time to make themselves familiar with Amy's background. If they'd wanted to. They'd simply not bothered. She wondered if she should tell him about Amy's having been a nurse. For her own part, Theodora couldn't really see Amy, small and frail as she was, physically assaulting anyone, not so as to kill them.

'Perhaps we could start,' Spruce was saying, 'with Mr Marr. Could you tell us what his background might be? For example, we really need to know about his previous and current experience, his strengths and weaknesses, his relationships in his job and with his wife, whether he had any problems, any enemies. Was he in general, would you say, well-liked, regarded as a competent priest?'

The Archdeacon looked at the Inspector kindly, as at a son who has much to learn.

'We don't do things in the church quite in the way that the form of your questions presupposes, Inspector,' he said crisply. 'The patronage system . . .' he began, and then turned to the Bishop.

'What the Archdeacon means is that the way in which priests are appointed means that the sort of questions which you are asking, while perfectly appropriate for an appointment in commerce or industry or indeed other professions, simply don't apply in the Church. If the patron of a living, in this case of course, Lord Dersingham, wants to put in a particular cleric, and if there is nothing, as it were, against that cleric for the Bishop to object to, then in he goes.'

'You have to induct?'

'Yes. Yes. On the whole.'

'What would a Bishop feel he had a right to object to?'

'Well, sexual deviance is not usually tolerated, and any conviction for a criminal offence. Though, of course, it would depend on the nature of that offence. The law of God and the law of man . . .'

'You mean if he were a homosexual, he'd be barred?'

There was communal hesitation.

Had Hereward Marr been homosexual, Theodora wondered? That was not what she had inferred from Amy's vehement if disjointed revelations. But that, of course, was not conclusive. Certainly her impression was that Amy and Hereward had not enjoyed a full sexual life.

'Was any check made on Mr Marr before he was inducted?'

'It would be unusual to question the patron's choice,' said the Bishop regretfully.

'Can you give me any help with his family background and previous career?' said the Inspector, turning from the unresolvable.

The Archdeacon had an inspiration. '*Crockford*!' he said, and appeared to be about to go in search.

Theodora bit her lip to restrain her grin. She glanced at Spruce to see how he would react. But he kept his gaze level and his tone when he replied was perfectly courteous. 'I've had a look at *Crockford*. I've got the bare bones, but I'm not too sure about the interpretation of detail,' Was the Inspector being disingenuous, Theodora wondered.

'D would mean . . . ?'

'Deacon,' said the Bishop, happy to be able to help the uninitiated.

'Well, the first thing I noticed is that it omits the date of birth. Would you have any idea how old Mr Marr might be?'

'I put him in his early fifties,' said the Archdeacon judiciously. 'It could be inferred from the date of university graduation, provided of course, that he went up at the usual time.'

Spruce nodded and, reading from his notebook, continued, 'So it runs: Educated privately; 1960, Emmanuel College, Cambridge, BA Modern Languages, Tripos part two 2.ii; 1961, Deacon; 1962, P, that would be . . . ?'

'Priested. Made a . . . Yes.' The Bishop nodded encouragingly.

The Inspector pushed on through the unfamiliar undergrowth, '1965 to 1972, Priest in charge, St James's Malta; 1973 to 1980, Priest in charge, St George's Monte Regia; 1982 to 1987, Vicar of St Ermyntrude Warnford Parva; 1987, Rector, St Benet Oldfield with St Nicholas Nether Oldfield.' The Inspector paused. 'I wonder if I could ask you to comment on that as a career structure,' he said levelly.

Theodora suspected that this was not an exercise that either the Bishop or the Archdeacon had had to perform before. However they rose manfully to the challenge, each in his own way.

'An overseas ministry is by no means a second-rate one. And I see he read Modern Languages,' said the Bishop with the complacency of someone making a sound inference, 'which would doubtless be a help to him.'

'Someone must have known him at Emmanuel,' added the Archdeacon. 'On the other hand, I see he doesn't mention the name of his theological college. Of course, there was a bit of a shakeout in the mid-seventies and a fair number disappeared, which might explain . . .'

Theodora spoke for the first time. 'There appears to be a lacuna between finishing his cure at Monte Regia and coming to St Ermyntrude's.'

The Inspector turned to her for the first time, but if he was cheered by her observation he gave no sign of his approval. 'How could I find out what he was doing between 1980 and 1982?' he asked.

'Warnford might know,' said the Archdeacon, 'Oh no, he wouldn't, of course. Dropped dead at the Royal Norfolk show last month. Very sudden. No heir, estate to be sold.'

'Who would Mr Marr's superior have been when he was in the overseas ministry?'

'Italy? Bishop of Gibraltar, or rather Bishop of Gibraltar in Europe as he's called nowadays,' supplied the Archdeacon. 'He's in Tonbridge Wells at the moment for the ecumenical conference.'

'Of course.' The Inspector made a meticulous note. 'And he would know?'

'He might. He might indeed,' said the Bishop heartily.

'Would the fact that he was put in as priest at Oldfield mean that Marr would have to have been known to Lord Dersingham?'

'Well, acceptable to him, certainly,' said the Bishop. 'I don't know whether Dersingham knew him prior to his appointing him. You will presumably ask him.'

'I just wanted to check the ecclesiastical forms before I approached Lord Dersingham,' said the Inspector. 'Could we turn to his work in this Parish? How would he have been assessed? Had he any problems, for example?'

Each took his own way through this one. 'Well,' said the Archdeacon, 'he wouldn't have been assessed in any very formal sense. Though, of course, both the Bishop and I "visit", as we put it. However, those are occasions more for boosting morale than for scrutinising the operations of a parish.'

'I think you have to remember that the priestly ministry is one which makes considerable demands, both emotional and spiritual, on its members,' the Bishop added.

The Inspector nodded respectfully. 'Had there been a visitation either by your lordship or by the Archdeacon since Mr Marr took up his appointment?'

'Well hardly. He'd only been in eighteen months,' said the Bishop, in the manner of a man who is used to a longer temporal perspective.

The Inspector made a note. 'So you might not have known if the Rector was under any special strain?'

It was apparent to Theodora, if not to the Inspector, that they simply did not know. They were proceeding by reflex, the Bishop to protect his clergy, the Archdeacon to protect his system. Gossip they would have heard fast and in copious quantities, but a more systematic set of information they did not possess.

'So, as far as you know, he had no special problems? He did not drink, for example?'

'Not beyond what he could hold,' said the Archdeacon firmly, as though stamping on a particularly pernicious untruth.

'Do we know who his friends were or whether he had any enemies?'

The Bishop was able to cope with this. 'I'm sure you know, Inspector, how impossible it is for even the most committed clergy to avoid incurring — not to put too fine a point on it — hatred. Indeed whole parishes sometimes, I'm sorry to say, gang up on their clergy. I always warn my men that there's something of the scapegoat involved in the role of parish priest. As our Lord, so his servants.'

'Was there anyone special known to you, Bishop?'

'Oh, I don't think so, do you Dick? Nothing at all out of the ordinary. Small communities get things out of perspective. That's where we come in. We can afford to take both a larger and longer view. Keep things ticking over on an even keel.' The Bishop outlined his view of the Kingdom of God.

Theodora watched the Inspector's face. She admired him for betraying neither bafflement nor contempt.

The Inspector tried again. 'What about his marriage? Would you have any information about that?' If Spruce was ironic it was in the words not the tone.

Immediately, an atmosphere of pastoral seriousness joined the two senior clergy together: here at least they were on their own ground.

'I think we were aware of strains,' the Archdeacon conceded.

'The role of a priest's wife can be stressful,' the Bishop elaborated. 'Some wives develop a ministry of their own. The Mothers' Union and so on. Others find fulfilment in the loving support of their husbands. It's not always easy. We do know that.'

The Inspector failed to find the theology of women's ministry in the church interesting. He made another attempt to lever the odd concrete fact from the slippery pair. 'Was Mrs Marr living at the Rectory?'

'I rather think,' said the Archdeacon detachedly, 'that for the last couple of months she had merely visited.'

'Where was she living?'

'I regret, I can't help you there but' — the Archdeacon turned to Theodora with his courteous smile — 'I believe you may be able to, Miss Braithwaite.' Having ignored her for forty minutes while they failed to answer questions about Amy to which she might know the answer, Theodora might perhaps have been forgiven for telling them nothing. But she felt no rancour. She knew that junior deacons in their second curacies, even if they came from distinguished clerical families, were not expected to make contributions uninvited when in the presence of very senior clergy. She understood the system. She had weighed its strengths and weaknesses. So now Theodora looked across at the Inspector, wondering just how much she was prepared to say to this man. Gilbert Racy's words came back to her. On balance, she felt enough loyalty to Gilbert and enough concern about Amy to feel that, if she were alive and if she were by any chance a party to her husband's death, the Church rather than the police should be her first sanctuary. She could not betray that sanctuary. With only a very slight hesitation she launched into her part. She told Spruce more or less what she'd told the Archdeacon of her contact with Mrs Marr in London at St Sylvester's Betterhouse, mentioning Racy without revealing that he'd phoned her on Sunday.

Spruce took down the names she gave him without comment. 'So you don't know anything of Mrs Marr's background, where she came from, who her friends were?'

'We don't ask clients to reveal any more about themselves than they want. Amy didn't, at any rate to me, give any of the sort of information you've mentioned. All I can tell you is that Amy was in St Benet Oldfield on Friday night.' And Theodora recounted her meeting with her in the drive at the Julians' house.

'Is that the last you saw of Mrs Marr?'

Theodora hesitated. 'If you mean, did I see her again either before her car was submerged or after that had happened, no.'

'But?'

Theodora was aware of the strength of Spruce's attention, but it wasn't aggressive, merely professional, and she in no way resented it. 'At some point,' she said, 'Amy left her wedding ring in the Dersingham chapel of St Benet Oldfield.'

'How do you mean?'

'I visited the chapel on Sunday afternoon,' Theodora said, 'and found it there.'

'How did you know it was Mrs Marr's?'

'Most wedding rings are plain or, if engraved, are so on the inside. Amy's was engraved on the outside, HM*AM. When she spoke of her marriage on one occasion at one of our sessions, she referred to her feelings towards it as those which one might entertain towards a manacle.'

There was a silence. All became aware that the Inspector had been writing fast. Finally he looked up from his notebook. 'So where is it now?'

'I left it,' said Theodora, 'on the thirteenth-century Lady Dersingham's stone finger.'

* * *

As the door closed behind the Inspector the atmosphere lightened.

'Coffee,' said the Archdeacon hungrily, and rang the bell beside the fireplace for his wife. The Bishop gazed at his defunct colonial colleague in the portrait over the mantelpiece. On the live Bishop the silver pectoral cross rose and fell on the purple cassock. Theodora got up in the expectation of being dismissed. The Bishop waved her back to her seat.

'I was wondering,' he glanced at the Archdeacon, 'if, in the light of the thrust, as it were, of the police's questioning, whether it might not be a prudent move if we filled in one or two blank spots in our intelligence about Hereward and, of course, Amy.'

A woman, thought Theodora, whom he'd met once.

'Miss Braithwaite,' he turned towards her with warmth, 'I realise of course that you're on holiday and I hate to intrude on your leisure, but since you have some knowledge already, I wonder, would you feel able, discreetly, of course, to make one or two enquiries? And if Amy is in need of help and if you were able to locate her, I think we'd all be inestimably in your debt.'

His tone conveyed that he did not consider Theodora had much option but to accept.

* * *

'Learn anything?' asked his driver, as Spruce eased himself into the Datsun.

'Only about the way they run the Church of England,' said the Inspector bitterly.

He thought of his own rigorous training, the constant reports on his work and conduct which followed him from computer base to computer base. The examinations for sergeant, for Inspector, the health checks, the interviews with senior officers, the specialist courses. Odd to give the spiritual leadership of three villages to a man about whom you knew nothing, who appeared to have received minimum training, whose fitness no one seemed concerned to have established, whose career wasn't even recorded. He shook his head impatiently.

'Just give Nether Oldfield a buzz and tell them to close St Benet Church and put a man back on it till we can get down there,' he ordered as they drew out of the cathedral close, under the Dersingham arch.

CHAPTER SEVEN: DOCTOR MAINGAY

In the garden of the Adam and Eve, Theodora drank sherry and gave herself the pleasure of gazing at the spire of the cathedral. She reflected on the Church of England and its structures. She knew, of course, had known from the cradle, that the Church as a worldly institution attempted too much and was, for just that reason, the more spectacular in its shortcomings; was, in fact, absurd. 'Be all things to all men', St Paul had unwisely written. And in its attempts to obey, the Anglican branch had evolved ad hoc, adding to itself bits and pieces to meet needs it thought it perceived. Nothing was ever dropped. As with cathedral buildings, time was entrusted with the task of seasoning and moulding the diverse parts into a harmonious whole. But whatever might be achieved in architecture by such methods, in an organisation the results were less satisfactory. Those who liked that sort of thing spoke of organic growth, those who did not murmured 'shambles'. Above all, Theodora blushed at the memory of the conversation with the Inspector. It was true, they didn't have any ways of making sure that clergy did their job. It was quite possible for them to take their deferences and privileges and give rather little in return. Only after they were dead, it seemed, did the hierarchy begin to enquire into performance. And any enquiry instantly illuminated the incompetence and, she had to admit it, the dishonesty, of that hierarchy. They covered their complacent idleness and ignorance with theological catch-phrases which could not excuse a lack of grasp. Perhaps, thought Theodora dispassionately, it was time they had to answer advertisements for their posts, satisfy a set of agreed criteria and become answerable to those who paid for their upkeep. Left as they were, they were not just incompetent but dangerous.

She contrasted their showing with Inspector Spruce. She'd rather admired the man. He'd been patronised and shown no resentment. He'd been evaded and had persevered. Moreover, he knew and respected Laura Maingay, clearly a recommendation. She found herself regretting she'd not been entirely open with him. It was not so much that she did not trust him as that she had been inhibited by her clerical superiors, Gilbert included. And though the Bishop and Treadwell had asked her to their meeting, they hadn't really invited her to say what she knew. So she hadn't mentioned Gilbert's phone call about Amy being alive on Saturday evening or Amy's talk of a box. She suspected that the Bishop and the Archdeacon had invited her to the meeting more to enlist her help as a sleuth than as a source of information of a kind which might be, to them in any case, unwelcome. Ought she to seek Spruce out and tell him what she knew? She'd think about it. Loyalty to her clerical superiors, to the Church and all it stood for, battled with her contempt for the way in which the senior clergy had behaved both to herself and to Amy. But as long as there was a chance of helping Amy, Theodora resolved she would do her best, even if this meant an encroachment on her precious holiday.

After the departure of the policeman, the Bishop had been practical to the point of explicitness.

'We don't of course need to duplicate the police enquiries about Mrs . . . Amy's movements immediately prior to Hereward's death,' he'd said. 'I've no doubt they're perfectly competent at that sort of thing. We do need to know rather more about her background than our own records apparently give us.' He'd looked meaningfully at Treadwell. The Bishop was not above playing the favourite game of the clergy, the blame game. Archdeacons were supposed to have what information was available. Having secured Theodora's obedience, however, he left it to the Archdeacon to make his wishes clear. 'I don't think we need take up more of your precious time, Miss Braithwaite,' he'd concluded. 'You'll keep us in the picture, won't you?'

The Bishop having departed, Treadwell had walked Theodora down the short drive of his handsome house.

'You want me,' Theodora had enquired, 'to research the "background", as it were, of Mr and Mrs Marr?' Theodora's tone was so gentle, so unemphatic, almost deferential — the tone of a deacon of four years' experience to a senior cleric of thirty years — that it took the edge off her words.

'I think the Bishop feels it would help us to be a little more fully informed. In the circumstances.'

It was on the tip of Theodora's tongue to point out that the networks of bishops were ten times as extensive as those of deacons, even deacons from clerical families. Even if they had no records and hadn't bothered to enquire before they inducted the man, surely they were better placed than she was. But she remained silent.

The Archdeacon may have divined something of her thought. 'Hereward was rather an oddity,' he said apologetically. 'He had a considerable presence. He acted as though he was very important, as though he expected to be treated differently from — indeed better than — anyone else. He used rather old-fashioned diction and made a parade of old-fashioned manners. But he did it in a way which seemed to belittle others. On the odd occasions I met him, I felt that he'd adopted all these trappings to keep off a world with which he could not cope. He wanted it on his own terms. Which, of course,' said the Archdeacon, a genuinely humble man, 'we cannot have. He wasn't, you know, just a lovable eccentric. I felt that there was something, well, really rather unpleasant about him. But it would look a little odd if we were to start an official inquiry into his origins and background now. I mean, we've left it rather late.'

Theodora admired his honesty.

He went on. 'After all, you've a connection with Amy through Gilbert Racy and St Sylvester's which is really most fortuitous.'

Theodora smiled to herself. It wasn't the first time in the Church and especially amongst the orthodoxly successful echelons of bishops and archdeacons, that Theodora had met a reluctance to tangle with that eminence grise, Gilbert Racy. The traditional suspicion of the regular clergy for members of the monastic orders, and the contempt that the latter often returned them might, she reflected, be reason enough to explain her enlistment.

Theodora's eye reached the top of the spire as she drank the last of the sherry. Was it, she wondered, back at St Sylvester's that the heart of her investigation lay? She made one final attempt on the Archdeacon before departing. 'Is there any help at all you can give me, Mr Treadwell, on either Amy or Hereward?' she'd asked. 'When you say that Hereward was unpleasant, for example, what had you in mind?'

'I wish I could be more explicit. It really is no more than intuition. The sort of thing one scents rather than actually sees. That house, for example. You remember?'

Theodora remembered.

'I had hoped that Bishop Julian or perhaps Rosalind might be of use here. But . . .'

'They won't be back for another ten days.'

'I think,' said the Archdeacon, 'that the Bishop's hoping for some movement before that. In fact, fairly soon.'

In fact, thought Theodora, before either the police or the press find out anything which could harm the Church.

'What I can do,' the Archdeacon was saying in a tone of inspiration, 'is pass you the St Benet Oldfield parish file. I feel sure there'd be no objection to that. If you like to look back at the cathedral office in an hour, I'll see it's ready for you. However,' and here Treadwell's toad-like features broke into his genuine kind smile. 'I have absolute confidence in you, Miss Braithwaite. I knew your father.'

Had Theodora not been her father's daughter, and therefore beautifully bred, she might have snorted at such palpable idiocy.

'And, of course,' the Archdeacon was continuing, 'if you should incur any expenses in the course of your enquiries, the diocese will be happy to reimburse you. The diocesan mileage allowance, by the way, is thirty pence a mile for cars over 1,000 cc.' Courteously he had opened the gate for her. 'I do hope you'll find time to see something of our beautiful city. It's a fine city, Norwich.'

* * *

Laura Maingay put a bookmark into the spring number of the Henry Doubleday Research Institute Quarterly at 'Experiments with Brassicas in Non-organic and Organic Beds'. The answerphone message had said 4.30. It had not perhaps been entirely a surprise but certainly a delight. So much to talk about, to catch up on.

Doctor Maingay regarded herself as a resource for others. Her job, her leisure, her religion were devoted to being a provider of, at best, health and knowledge, at the least of time or food. She was unmarried and her urge and talent for giving to the world had something of gratitude at its root. How marvellous it was to be free; how appalling it would have been to have had to wash some man's socks and cope with his whingeing children. She could never get over her lucky escapes. Donald, Hector, Alexander, Andrew, she ticked them off sometimes as a litany of fortunate deliverances. Instead, she was utterly at leisure to give unstintingly to friends and foes, colleagues and passing tramps. The doctor daughter of two doctors, her mother an Edinburgh Scot, she was well qualified to exercise her generosity, which was genuine and without end.

The doorbell rang. The awaited guest walked through the already open door. Theodora stood tall and handsome in the tiny modern hall. Thirty years apart in age, they embraced with that warmth of affection which pious women sometimes allow themselves towards each other, knowing that it will be mistaken for nothing else.

'My dear, such a time.'

'Laura, so long.'

'Your dear father.'

'I know. I can't tell you how I miss him.'

'I'm sure. Now come along, tea first. Go through.'

Theodora wound her way down the long narrow garden, bowing her head under the arching tendrils of the old roses, edging past the organic asparagus bed and avoiding the hazard of the flight paths of bees intent on making for their two hives. At the end, beneath a couple of mature coxes, was an iron table and stout wooden chairs. Nothing of Laura's would be flimsy.

Settling herself into her chair, Laura busied herself with pouring out tea.

'Now, tell me why and how.' The Lapsang scented the warm air.

'The Julians wanted a house — and cat-watcher. I'd had no leave and, what with one thing and another, I rather wanted a break. London is . . .'

'Terrible.' Laura finished her sentence triumphantly. 'And are you still with the ambiguous Gilbert?' she asked.

'Officially, I'm Geoffrey Brighouse's curate. But, so that I don't bankrupt the parish, I do a bit of teaching at St Veep's and the odd session for Gilbert. Why is he ambiguous?'

'My dear, I've known Gilbert Racy for thirty years. I knew him when he had holes in his socks as a post-graduate. And before that we were fellow medics at Barts.'

'I thought his doctorate was in psychology.' Theodora was beginning to realise how little she knew about Gilbert.

'Swapped after his first MB. Real medicine didn't interest him. Too much like hard work. Or, as he would put it, material causes too crude and not ultimately explanatory, mental causes more refined.'

'When did he transform mental causality into spiritual?' Theodora was curious.

'He had some sort of breakdown just before he was due to present. I was much too busy doing my dreadful houseman's year to notice what was happening. I never really got the full story. But I gather he went to see Matthew Jacob who suggested St Sylvester's. He spent three months there and came out a changed man. He completed, took orders and entered the novitiate all within a couple of years. Never one to hang about, Gilbert, once he'd made up his mind.'

'I still don't see why you think he's ambiguous.'

'Surely, if you've worked for him you must know what I mean.' Laura sounded genuinely surprised.

'I find him intellectually very able.'

Theodora was cautious. She did not add that this was quite a relief amongst the Anglican priesthood. Nevertheless, she had been forced to agree with Geoffrey, her vicar, when, after a local deanery chapter meeting, he'd said that a stranger might be forgiven for supposing that the Church of England in south London was staffed by middle-aged ex-lorry drivers, recruited via the Southwark Ordination Course, plus a sprinkling of very young men who had found their accountancy examinations too arduous. In such a setting Gilbert, Geoffrey had concluded, in a rare flight, glowed like a day lily in a border of salvias.

'Perhaps ambiguous isn't quite right,' Laura conceded. 'More . . . divided.'

'How divided?' Theodora was aware that she was asking Laura to clarify her own feelings about Gilbert. How *did* she feel about him? Was he trustworthy as well as intelligent? Laura, she reflected, was as likely to help her as anyone.

'He's able, as you say,' Laura went on, 'but wouldn't finish a medical course. He's a sybarite who joined an order which has poverty as one of its vows. He's attracted and attractive to women and, I'd guess, to men too, and yet he lives as a celibate. He's perfectly worldly, knows how systems work, but chooses to act as though they don't matter.'

Theodora listened to Laura's dry dissecting tone with its merest hint of her mother's Edinburgh accent. Hadn't she just described the truly religious man, someone in the world but not of it? She heard again Gilbert's voice down the phone. 'The souls of the dead are in the hands of God,' he'd said. She also reflected that Laura seemed to know a fair amount about Gilbert.

'Do you keep up with him?' She wondered just how up-to-date Laura's knowledge of Gilbert was.

'Christmas and ordination anniversary,' replied Laura matter-of-factly. 'But in fact the Society has a sister house outside Diss. Sisters of the Society of St Sylvester.'

'Of course.' Theodora dimly recalled Rosalind having mentioned it. 'He makes his Lent retreat there, doesn't he?'

'Right. Our sojourns there have sometimes coincided.' Laura's tone was dry.

Theodora paused to speculate how, since a Holy Week retreat at St Sylvester's would almost certainly be conducted in silence, these two communicated with each other. Easter Sunday must have been noisy. She put aside this interesting thought and took the plunge. 'Laura, I have actually come for your help.'

Laura felt that familiar warm glow. Once more her life was to be justified. She could exercise her talent. 'Hereward Marr and Amy,' she said with pleasure, replenishing the cups.

Theodora raised an eyebrow. 'How did you know? Has Gilbert rung?'

'Gracious no. We're not on those terms. No, I did the post-mortem on Hereward.' Inspector Spruce and I are old friends. I do the odd body for him when he's desperate.'

'And?'

'Not in good shape. Terrible liver.' Laura spoke with all the complacency of the truly healthy.

'No, I mean, why was he killed? That's what the police are asking us.'

'Us?'

'Well, the Church.' Theodora described the meeting of the Bishop and Archdeacon with the Inspector. 'So you see, what with the Church never keeping adequate records and relying on the personal network all the time and the patronage system doing the same but relying on a different network, we're all rather in the dark.'

Laura was amused. 'It's nice to find the Church hoisted by its own petard for once. Time they had a General Medical Council keeping tabs on them, like the rest of us. So, they've hired you for thirty pence a mile to do their roadwork for them. I like thirty, it has a history, I seem to remember. Are you supposed to find out who killed Hereward or where Amy is?'

'I think the Church are supposing it would be one and the same.'

'You sound as though you don't make the same inference.'

Theodora recounted to Laura the phone call she had had from Gilbert Racy and her own finding of the wedding ring in the Dersingham chapel of St Benet Oldfield.

'That seems to me rather to reinforce suspicion that Amy killed Hereward,' Laura said.

'Oh I admit she had a motive. The marriage stank.'

It was Laura's turn to raise an eyebrow. Theodora was not given to hyperbole.

'She came to us at St Sylvester's,' Theodora amplified.

'Gilbert's very discreet group for battered clergy wives.'

'You knew?'

'I didn't know Amy was a client. I knew Gilbert dabbled in marriage therapy.'

'Dabbled?'

'Not being married, is, I think, a handicap in such cases.'

'He'd say it preserved perspective. Spiritual detachment.'

'He'd be wrong. How did it stink?'

'I gather Hereward had quite an accomplished line in undermining self-respect, making Amy and indeed others wonder if they were acceptable, passed muster. He was quite acute, if Amy was to be believed. He could sniff out the personal myth, the crucial one we all develop for ourselves, and make mincemeat of it.'

'What was Amy's myth?'

'Woman, wife and mother. I think. So he made sure she failed on all counts. No children, odd sex and, as a high churchman, he'd really have had a better image of himself if he'd managed to keep to celibacy. She had, by the time he'd finished with her, no place.'

Laura winced. Just what she felt marriage was likely to bring about. 'Why did she marry him?'

'I thought you might know about both of them.'

'I'm not sure how much use I can be to you. I met Amy occasionally at the House, when I was attending one of the servants, a chauffeur called Yaxlee. She used to visit him.'

'Where did Amy come from?'

'I think I heard it said they met in Italy.'

'And before that?'

Laura shrugged, 'Not his class, at all events.'

'And what was his class? Where did he come from?'

'I can't say for certain. He used to carry on as though he were on a level with Dersingham. I stumbled over him when he was visiting Ted Yaxlee. It was towards the end of poor old Ted's time. He was there, hoping for a death bed. Something of a speciality of his I gather.'

'Look, Laura, I really need to be clear about one or two things before I can see my way forward.'

'Fire away then,' said Laura happily.

'First, can I trust Inspector Spruce?'

'Yes,' said Laura decisively. 'I've known him since he was a sergeant. When I first went in for forensic medicine he used me a lot and I got a great deal of experience I wouldn't otherwise have had because he was never too proud to ask for a specialist opinion. He's the very best. Intelligent, humane, absolutely straight. Why do you want to know?'

'Well, I wasn't entirely open with him at the Archdeacon's meeting. I was worried about what I should be saying, or about what Gilbert would think I should — or shouldn't — be saying. I told Spruce a bit about Amy and Hereward's marriage and I did mention that I'd seen her here on Friday night and Saturday morning. What I didn't mention to him was Gilbert's phone call where he said she rang him on Saturday evening and asked him about a box.'

Laura ruminated. 'I can think of two other people who might want Hereward dead.'

Theodora waited.

Laura paused for a moment before she responded. Then she said, 'Both Dersingham and Vanessa could have motives for wanting Hereward dead.' She looked a bit uncomfortable, from which Theodora inferred that she too was going to divulge professional information. And so it proved.

'You should understand' — the Edinburgh tone was now quite unmistakable — 'that I don't know either Dersingham or his sister at all well. They've never been patients of mine, though, as I say, I have done some of the servants and villagers. But my father attended the old Baron in his last illness. I was about eleven at the time, it must have been just after the war. The eldest boy, Leopold, did you know, hanged himself round about 1942.'

Theodora nodded.

'And the eldest girl . . .'

'Killed over fences.'

'Just so. Well, I remember my father saying of the old Baron that in his last illness he talked all the time of there being a grandson. But of course, none of the children had ever married. So, either the old man was thinking wishfully or there was a bastard, or the product of an unacknowledged marriage.'

'So how does this connect with Hereward?'

'It may not. But I can remember my father coming back from the death bed and saying the old man was babbling about a grandson. I wondered if there *was* a boy in fact, and whether Hereward knew something about him,' Laura finished off.

'If Leopold had had a son, would it be the heir?' Theodora asked.

'It would depend if he were legitimate, wouldn't it?'

'If he were,' said Theodora thoughtfully, 'where would that leave the present Baron, Louis and his sister?'

'Out in the cold. Yes?'

'You mean Hereward might have known something which Dersingham needed to keep quiet about?'

'Hereward frequented death beds and heard confession. He might pick up a truth or two perhaps from servants or villagers of the Old Baron's generation.'

Theodora was shocked. 'It would be a dreadful abuse of the sacrament,' she said, 'but I wonder if it might explain why Dersingham gave Hereward the living, which' — she concluded — 'everyone seems to agree, needs some explanation. And there's another point. The Archdeacon said Louis had spent a fortune trying to trace an heir.'

'Did he, did he indeed?' Laura's eye lit up. She had read Sir Walter Scott all her life.

'How difficult for poor Louis,' Laura said. 'He wants an heir but not one who would disinherit *him* presumably. So if Hereward did turn up one who would threaten his inheritance, he might want to keep it, and Hereward, quiet.'

'He might. On the other hand . . .'

'On the other hand' — Laura was now well into the possible permutations — 'Louis is getting on. He might feel that any heir, even one who disinherits him, is worth having so long as it keeps the name going.'

'What would Vanessa feel about that, would you say?' Theodora enquired tentatively.

'Absolutely a closed book to me,' Laura admitted. 'But being a woman and not able to inherit, I suppose she might be used to being a second string. She's been one all her life. So she might not be bothered if Louis lost his place to an heir. It depends how she feels about Louis.'

Theodora totted up. 'Amy might want Hereward dead, even if she did not kill him herself, so perhaps I need to know where Amy is now, whether she's alive or dead. Hereward's own background needs clarifying in case there are other people who wanted him dead. Dersingham, and by extension Vanessa, might have a motive, so I need to know where he's got to in his search for a putative heir. There's going to be a lot to do for a holiday.'

'We can divide the chores between us,' said Dr Maingay with enthusiasm. 'I'll take the medical, you deal with the Church.'

CHAPTER EIGHT: MRS YAXLEE

Mrs Yaxlee had grown unused to entertaining. Indeed it had never been a favourite pastime of hers. She tended to do it of late years by proxy, as it were: she was good — or had been before the advent of the Reverend Hereward Marr — at manning the tea urn at the church social. That should suffice for her social obligations, she felt. And what with her heart and now her leg, she felt fully excused from all effort in that area. Family, however, she allowed, was different. George was her grandson. His dad hadn't much luck dying in his fifties and the boy had looked in with the bread and milk most days since her accident. She had been surprised when he'd come round after supper on Sunday and asked if he could bring his new friend to tea the next day. She'd not been able to think what to say. If Deaconess Tilley hadn't been there at the time, she might have found an excuse to say no. But Deaconess Tilley had said, 'Go on, Mrs Y. It'll do you good to see a fresh face. Bit of life. Push the boat out.'

It wasn't any of the Deaconess's business, but Mrs Yaxlee had been swayed by the fact, made evident in George's expression, that he expected her to refuse.

'You can bring him Monday tea-time, if you want,' she said.

And George, recognising a very high order of warmth on his grandmother's part, had thanked her very much.

'He's very interesting,' he'd begun to say in his relief, and then stopped. There was no point in frightening his grandmother before time.

'He knows about horses,' he ended safely.

Deaconess Tilley's notions of the food proper for entertaining was formed from the needs of large families on small incomes crossed with Church 'does' of various kinds. They coincided with Mrs Yaxlee's own ideas closely enough for the latter to trust her to do the shopping while at the same time failing to include her in the invitation which she so palpably wanted. So, at half-past five on Monday evening, George and Leon, edging their way round the matchboard door, found baps filled with fish paste and a nice square mottled chunk of bought cherry cake, washed down with deep orange-coloured Indian tea, to nourish them.

The boys' physical presence was rendered huge by the small room. They sat round the square oak table wedged against the wall and consumed the tea. George ate with the complete concentration of a boy who was still growing. Leon, more conscious of his status as guest, put away a fair amount less overtly. He had deeply embarrassed Mrs Yaxlee by presenting her on his arrival with a delicate linen handkerchief, beautifully wrapped in pink tissue paper. However, she had recovered manfully from this shock and, though infirm in leg, nevertheless flexed her ample arm easily enough to lift the immense tea-pot and replenish at frequent intervals the capable-looking tea-cups.

George's fears about conversation turned out to be exaggerated. Talk ranged widely. Mrs Yaxlee was not greatly travelled: Yarmouth had sufficed in youth; London had never entertained her. But she was genuinely curious about the young Italian. She recalled the Italian prisoners-of-war in their unsoldierly uniforms who had worked on the estate for a time towards the end of the war; she made civil mention of another of Leon's countrymen who had sold ice-cream on Norwich market when she was a girl.

'So what does your dad do?' Mrs Yaxlee asked Leon when the eating died down.

Leon had met this one before. He described their house, the large stable which had grown year by year under the assiduous management of his father, or 'second father', as he hesitatingly described him.

'Stepfather?' suggested George.

Leon nodded gratefully.

'What's your part of the country like then?' pursued Mrs Yaxlee who, once embarked on her hostessly duties, followed them to the end.

'The country is not like here. There are many woods and mountains. Our house is on a small hill which looks towards the large hill, Monte Regia. It is good for horse to exercise up hills. So we have many strong horses. We breed them for the course, especially and also now for the sport.' Leon had done this bit before. But, warmed by the fish baps and sweet tea, he wished to offer more of his home to his kind friends than he had previously rehearsed. He pressed on.

'We live in great happiness there. My two sisters are younger than me and my mother and my second . . .' he hesitated 'my . . .'

'Stepfather,' said George again.

'Yes.'

'If he's not your dad, he must be your stepfather.'

'Yes. So. My father was killed by his auto when I was four years. So I do not know him well. My mother then married my second, step, father quite early. It is enough,' he concluded in triumph, though whether by way of verdict on his mother's marital mores or as comment on his own wrestling with the English language was not clear.

'I'm the other way,' said George companionably. 'My mum died when I was four. My dad didn't marry again.'

Mrs Yaxlee kept her counsel on that one. 'Better to marry too much than not at all,' she said cryptically.

Leon turned politely to George. 'So what will you do to live? You will serve your great family for ever?'

George set his face away from the prospect. 'Don't reckon they'll last long,' he said, more in hope than in prescience.

'They have no sons?' said Leon with genuine concern.

'Never been breeders,' Mrs Yaxlee said grimly.

'But the old *signorina* has a very good eye for a horse,' said Leon, as though there might be a connection between judging horse flesh and marrying.

'Better for a horse than for a man,' said Mrs Yaxlee with relish.

'The future will not be a great one without a family,' said Leon with the wisdom of seventeen years.

'They haven't always been as poor as they are now,' asserted George, beginning, to his surprise, to feel the stirrings of loyalty or pity for the Dersinghams. After all, he reasoned, they were his bread and butter, they were his and his family's family.

'Ah yes,' Leon turned to Mrs Yaxlee, 'your George has told me of the great days. The remarkable travel in the coach to the coronation of the King.'

George recognised his cue and took it up, 'We wondered if we might see the pictures and the tack. And the livery, my grandad's livery?'

Mrs Yaxlee's fin-like hand gestured in the direction of the dresser. 'The photo's in the album. Where the suit is, that I don't know.'

'You always said it was in the trunk, gran. Look, I'll get it. You don't have to stir yourself.'

If Mrs Yaxlee had a mind to veto this, George pre-empted her. He edged from the room as swiftly as the impeding furniture would let him, through the door which led straight onto the staircase to the upper storey.

Mrs Yaxlee looked at Leon, 'You want to see the pictures, then?'

'It would give great pleasure, *signora*, if you would allow me.' Leon hauled the heavy album from its position.

Mrs Yaxlee turned the pages with sufficient sense of drama to provide a build up. 'That's the family, then.' Her yellow nail traced once more for a stranger's benefit the blank faces, wide staring eyes of the previous generation of Dersinghams. 'That's Mr Louis, that's Mr Leopold, that's Miss Vanessa, that's Miss Victoria.'

'And the man in the middle of them?'

'That's the old Baron'.

'Where is his lady?'

'Her ladyship was dead, drowned, by that time,' said Mrs Yaxlee with relish.

'Ah, it is a family rich in ill-fortune,' intoned Leon, entering into the spirit of things with ease. He was a sympathetic boy, Mrs Yaxlee felt.

Leon gazed intently at the line of adolescent faces. 'They are very the same, the sisters, and the brothers, too, are alike.'

'Yes, well, all one family. You'd expect that.'

Mrs Yaxlee turned the page. 'And this is George's grandad with the horses.'

'And this is his grandson in his livery,' said George, appearing at the door with all the pleasure of an actor dead on cue. His audience swung round obediently. George's grandfather must have been a smaller man than George, for the brown livery was stretched across the shoulders and the boy's long wrists showed below the sleeve. There was a strong smell of moth-balls. Mrs Yaxlee gave her grandson a long considering look.

'You're not like your granda,' she said, 'and them days are gone anyway.'

George was not abashed. 'I've never worn a waistcoat before,' he said with pleasure. 'It's beautifully made. Look, it's got a buttonhole for a watch chain.' He pointed to the archaic foppery for Leon's benefit. But it was not at the buttonhole that Leon was looking. He bent forward and plucked at the coat.

'Hey, hang on,' said George partly in alarm. But Leon didn't let go, rubbing at the coat's tarnished silver button. Then from his own pocket he drew another, rather the same but very much shinier, and held it out in the palm of his hand.

'Well,' said Mrs Yaxlee, 'that's nice. Where'd you get that one then?'

* * *

'Father Gilbert's on holiday,' said the voice, a man's and unfamiliar to Theodora. She heard the words with despair. 'I didn't catch your name?' He waited expectantly. 'Theodora Braithwaite. I'm Geoffrey Brighouse's curate at St Sylvester's'.

'I regret to say,' said the voice with satisfaction, 'I've never heard of you.'

'I'm afraid I didn't catch *your* name,' said Theodora with spirit.

'I hardly think that it would help you if I were to give it.'

Theodora knew of old the willingness of the clergy to be far ruder over the phone than they would venture to be face to face. 'I wondered where Muriel was,' Theodora said hopefully, thinking with regret of the homely body in knitted Fair Isle bodices who usually manned Gilbert's phone.

'With her daughter who's having her third,' said the voice.

It sounded the sort of voice which might start offering gynaecological details if given half a chance. Theodora did not want to give it that chance. 'Can you tell me where I can get hold of Father Racy?'

The voice hesitated. Cheated of its medical outing, it clearly saw no reason to oblige. 'He left no address.'

'It's rather urgent. It's about one of his clients, Mrs Marr.'

'We've all got to have holidays. Time for refreshment of the spirit.'

'Ah, yes, indeed. Well, er, thank you.' Theodora knew when she'd met her match. 'If you should want to contact me, my number is Oldfield 214. Bishop Julian's house,' she added in a vain hope of pulling rank.

'Righty ho,' said the voice neutrally.

She replaced the phone in Bishop Julian's hall and stood for a moment indecisively. It was early evening. She'd left

Laura to the medical portion of their task. 'Come to lunch on Wednesday,' she'd pressed Laura as she left. 'We can pool finds.'

So, back to her Church bit. She recovered the parish file given her by the diocesan office and spread the meagre contents out on Bishop Julian's desk. Tobias came and sat on them. Theodora gently removed him. He returned. An Anglican compromise was reached: he sat on the ones she didn't need to read: baptismal returns (decreasing), adjustments of quota (increasing), confirmation numbers (decreasing). Theodora wondered if there was supposed to be an agreed format for this sort of information but failed to detect any. Such information as there was was typed in a number of different typefaces but all with fading ribbons. There was the trust deed of the church school, St Benet's, founded in 1860 and, of more recent date, a copy of a well-phrased vituperative complaint to the Archdeacon from the People's Warden about Marr's digging up the Church for the central heating. 'Godless desecration of the faithful departed. What will happen at the resurrection?' It had pertinently enquired. Yes indeed.

Theodora shuffled the documents and placed them ready for Tobias. There remained a couple of sheets of quarto. They appeared to be pages of an off-print of an article in a learned journal. Theodora glanced at the title. 'Confession and the Sacrament of Penance — the Pastoral Dimension'. It started with an historical perspective (Mark 1.14 and the Lateran Council of 1215), and ended with fashionable references to Bonhoeffer and Thurian. Idly Theodora turned to the last page. The author's name given at the end was the Reverend Hereward Marr, Associate of the Society of St Sylvester. Theodora gazed at the extraordinary, the unlooked-for information. When, she wondered, for how long, had Hereward Marr been connected with St Sylvester's?

Theodora reviewed what she knew about the Society of St Sylvester. The early history was familiar to her from the memoir of the founder which stood in limp green leather covers on Gilbert Racy's shelves at Betterhouse. The Society had been founded in the high noon of the Tracterian movement by the Reverend Thomas Henry Newcome, a Yorkshireman, a younger contemporary at Oxford of Father Faber. His means, though unmentioned, derived from his family's West Riding worsted mills, and were sufficient to give him a substantial independence from stipends. Perhaps influenced by the number of his contemporaries who showed neurasthenic tendencies, the Reverend Henry Newcome had founded a Society and formed a rule which had as its purpose the support of priests working in the growing parishes of newly industrialised cities. He had espoused, it seemed to Theodora, the very best in High Church practices, advocating the traditional techniques of the spiritual life as a means of keeping sane. Regular contemplative prayer, the use of liturgy and sacrament, the recourse to pilgrimage and retreat and the support of the like-minded in a brotherly community, had seemed to Newcome the very minimum foundations necessary to defeat the wiles of the devil which beset parochial clergy. That devil, born of isolation, he had seen so often destroy young men through exhaustion, frustration and despair. He had felt it the greatest lunacy to dispatch men to crowded city parishes with nothing more sustaining than goodwill, a knowledge of the learned tongues and an unrefined familiarity with the Bible. They needed practices of mind and ceremonies of the body which could sustain and calm the spirit.

The funds had run to two houses, one in London at Betterhouse on the south bank of the Thames, the other in the North Riding. Men had been trained; bishops (not many, but London and Oxford generally obliged) had been found willing to ordain to the priesthood. The priests had followed one of two paths: those who took the full vows of celibacy and poverty provided the staff at the houses dedicated to training the young priests; and those who, after their training, became associates and went into the parishes, to all intents and purposes no different from priests trained elsewhere. They were, nevertheless, men loyal to the catholic practices and theology of the Society.

As the new century had progressed, the catholic cause in the Anglican communion had fluctuated in line with the churchmanship of the two Archbishops. But the talents of a Society composed entirely of priests had, of later years, found the original insights of the founder fashionable again. Health of mind and soul, the inner realities, were once more beginning to be acknowledged. Even conventional medicine was starting to take the spirit, however unscientific a concept it might be, into account as a factor in the cause of bodily illness. A number of the members of St Sylvester were now doctors or psychologists as well as priests. They handed people, patients, on to each other, they were known and sought out by the desperate among both clergy and laity. They counselled, they supported, they lead retreats. They prayed both with and for the distressed. They were not quite a secret society but certainly a network, not always trusted, not, indeed, acceptable to some bishops and in some livings. But the work they did was, as far as Theodora could see, amongst the best the Church could offer. It aimed to meet, as only religion can, the most basic spiritual needs of people at the end of their tether. Her own reservations, which she admitted to no one and most of the time not fully even to herself, concerned their attitude to women and the laity. A church in which they predominated, would, she had to admit, have little place for such as she.

What, then, was Hereward doing amongst this specialised and refined body? Might the clue to his death be somehow discoverable from his association with the Society? She knew its subterranean power, its ability to command loyalty. She did not doubt but that somewhere amongst the records and corporate memory of the Society would be someone who knew Hereward Marr very well indeed. Would they also know who would want to kill him and why? And how could one such as she obtain such information?

Theodora sighed. What with the amateur incompetence of the diocesan authorities and the deliberate reclusiveness of the priestly Society, it was almost hopeless to suppose that such information might be recovered. She felt a brief pity for the police who would never pick their way through such a fen.

Theodora formed her resolution. She could go back to London and try and shake the whereabouts of Gilbert Racy out of his obstructive locum, or she could see what other members of the Society there were in Norfolk and glean what she might from them. There ought to be one or two.

It was nine-thirty. The light over the moated garden was fading fast. She reached for the phone. The Archdeacon was out, said his wife with courteous regret. Would she like to leave a message? Theodora did not feel up to framing one. Might she call again tomorrow? But of course, though not before ten-thirty as the Archdeacon was taking a matins for someone on holiday.

Theodora ran her eye along Bishop Julian's book shelves. Amongst the reference texts was a *Crockford*, a Diocesan Directory, *The Good Church Guide* and *The Care of Churchyards*. There was no list of members of the Society of St Sylvester, which, given Bishop Julian's churchmanship, hardly surprised her. She entertained but fleetingly the notion of ringing the Bishop. Curates in deacons' orders did not ask evangelical bishops how many of their clergy were of the catholic persuasion at half-past nine on August evenings, or indeed at any other time. There seemed to Theodora to be no help for it. She must brave the only place likely to have the information she wanted. With reluctance she pulled on a jacket and set out for the Rectory.

CHAPTER NINE: JEROME TOPSTOCK

Theodora stepped out into the warm air of the late summer evening. There was a smell of stubble and fen grass. Far off she heard the drone of a tractor working late or set for home. The Rectory, when she reached it ten minutes later, was as silent and calm as when she had visited it with the Archdeacon on Saturday evening. A late crow said a word as her entry through the open drive gate disturbed his first sleep. There was no other sound. She had seen Amy drive up to the house on Saturday morning. Had she then driven on here? And if so, why? And where had Amy been the previous night when her husband was being killed? Had she been in any way party to that act? Where had she spent Friday night? Above all, where was she now?

Theodora felt no fear at entering the house. She agreed with Gilbert that the souls of the dead are in the hand of God and, as for herself, she was persuaded that there is nothing in this world, or out of it, which can separate us from the love of God. Ghosts could ne'er affright her. After all, she and the Archdeacon had been into the house once already. She was more concerned about the police. They had, presumably, by now searched the Rectory? Had they done that after finding the car in the Broad or before? They couldn't have done it too promptly or else she and the Archdeacon would have met them after their ill-fated call on the Dersinghams. If the police had searched later, on the other hand, ought they not to have found her and Treadwell's fingerprints? But perhaps they simply hadn't been able to check out all the prints they'd found anyway. Ought she to have mentioned their visit to Spruce? She could hardly have done so without the Archdeacon's leave. She wondered whether he had mentioned it to the Inspector privately. Perhaps he had also mentioned the fact that they had observed Dersingham, presumably not too many hours after the discovery of the car in the Broad, with trousers which were dripping wet? Treadwell certainly hadn't mentioned any of this when Spruce had interviewed them with the Bishop. Could that have been clerical discretion, Theodora wondered, or clerical deviousness? Had he and the Bishop already decided even before Spruce came that they would set Theodora on (one, after all, of their own kind and bound by clerical obedience) rather than helping the normal, if crude, processes of the law? She realised, as she had mentioned to Laura, she was quite as guilty as her superiors of being less than open with the police. Perhaps she should try and see Spruce and put matters right. If Laura trusted him so should she. However, she put such thoughts aside for the moment and concentrated on the task in hand.

Would the police have left a man at the Rectory in case Amy returned? Not unfamiliar with the habits of police forces both in East Africa and West London, she felt it was, on balance, unlikely. There were never enough men for the work they had to do. Once they had made their inferences they tended to use any manpower they had to follow them up. If they thought that Amy was at the bottom of the Broad, they'd be dragging it. If, on the other hand, they thought she was alive, they would probably be checking the roads and railways to London and ports and airports to the continent. Either way, she felt it was worth taking a chance.

Theodora tried the front door. She remembered she and the Archdeacon had dropped the latch behind them. This time it did not yield. She surveyed the four ground-floor windows. Even if any of them was open they were all solid sash types which would have been heavy to raise from the outside. The one at the end, she noticed, was permanently open at the top, for creeper could be seen disappearing through the top light. But the bottom light, when she tried it, was stiff and would take more strength than she could summon to loosen it. She walked purposefully round the back. Here, abandoned domesticity was everywhere apparent. She all but tripped over a clothes line embedded in the tussocky grass. The ground was deeply cut up where Dersingham's cattle had been wont to stray. There were various shallow metal dishes scattered about and a wooden wheelbarrow with its vegetable remains pungent upon the night air. She skirted a hen house, not in its first youth but stalwart enough to keep out foxes. From it, as she passed, came the companionable muted clucking of hens settling for the night. Picking her way over the rough ground and through the hazards, she gained the kitchen entrance.

To the right of the back door, she found what she had hoped for, a Victorian window with a pane broken in the top light, leaving the catch within easy reach of someone of Theodora's height. Gently she released the metal bolt, eased up the lower light and clambered through. Inside the house it was darker and warmer than outside. She used Rosalind's flashlight to take her across the kitchen's frayed linoleum to the corridor. She stopped for a moment to get her bearings. Opposite her were two steps up to the baize door separating the kitchen quarters from the house. She pushed it open and entered the front hall. The familiar frowsty smell compounded of soot and chicken meal met her. The library, she remembered, was to the right, the dining room to the left. She struck out to the right, confident now, she was within reach of the object of her quest.

She visualised the copy of Cross's *Dictionary of the Christian Church* which she had noticed on her last visit. It seemed a fair inference that such reference books as Hereward

Marr possessed would be grouped together there. It was on the same wall as the door, to the left of it and just beside the telephone. She had decided not to risk using the electric light, even supposing the electricity was switched on, since a light from the front of the Rectory would be visible from the road and, therefore, news to the whole village. If there were police still about, they might well be roused to investigate. And although Theodora could think of no more innocent errand then her own, she knew from experience what a very long time the police require to digest even simple facts. She had no intention of spending the rest of the night answering questions.

Thus resolved, Theodora focused her flashlight on the brass doorknob on the panelled door. The door itself was ajar. Theodora allowed the beam to travel round the room. The first thing she saw was a hand, old, bent with arthritis, clutching a book. Even as she switched off her light, there came a low sibilant whistling; this was followed by something between a gargle and a hiccup. Theodora analysed the sounds. She had worked, during her training years, in enough down and out shelters to recognise without any trouble the sound of a drunk snoring.

Theodora was irritated: the irritation of someone upon whom demands were being made which would delay the completion of the enterprise in hand. Her general rule with regard to drunks was, let them lie. Her superiors in pastoral studies had, on the whole, been of the opinion it was not merely officious but often dangerous to move a drunk from the place he had chosen to lie down into one where he had not. Theodora was tempted. If some local traveller wanted to sleep it off in the Rectory, who was she to say he should not. Only one thing gave her pause. How had he got in? She'd looked for an opening and had had to contrive her entry. Surely she'd have noticed if there had been any other forced entry. It would be a superior tramp to have come in with a key. The snoring continued. With a sigh Theodora switched on her flashlight again, went softly down the room and played the beam cautiously round the sleeping figure. It was a man. His head was pillowed on his arm, his considerable bulk was sprawled across the floor with its litter of books as when Theodora had last seen it. In the frail beam of light the longish hair in separated locks gave an appearance of neglect almost greater than that suggested by his crushed trousers and crumpled jacket. Allowing herself a moment of pity, Theodora gazed down at the vulnerable sleeping figure. Poor Lord Dersingham. Out of curiosity, she let the light fall on the book doubled up under his elbow. It was a picture book in tattered paper covers: *The War in Norfolk*. Gently, Theodora removed it from his grasp. She listened to the breathing which, though stertorous was regular and, she judged, healthy. She decided she could safely leave him. She turned back to the left-hand side of the door and there, between Cross and the Diocesan Handbook, was the light green cover of the list of members of the Society of St Sylvester. Theodora's hand was already on it when the telephone shrilled. She had not realised how tense she had been until she jumped. With a single swift movement, almost by reflex, her only thought to prevent a second ring waking Dersingham, she picked up the receiver and put it to her ear.

'Hello,' said a familiar voice.

Theodora made no reply.

'Hello, Amy?'

Theodora had just drawn breath when she heard a click and the line went dead.

* * *

'Leg on. Leg on. Leg on.' Henry's voice carried without strain from one end of the paddock to the other. The neat, slight figure of the rider — Mrs Totteridge according to the stable girl — could be seen, square of shoulder, round of head, guiding a black mare through a triple.

Theodora watched the familiar scene from the comfort of her new mount, Roger, an enormous seventeen-hand chestnut with quarters like a tank, who, however, moved with a balanced and educated ease far different from that of the novice Cranmer. They had enjoyed each other's company over the last hour, hacking along the foreshore of the estuary. Then, entering Henry's land once more, they had taken a couple of fences in good style and returned home in excellent spirits, congratulating each other warmly.

Theodora dismounted and handed Roger to his silent stable girl. She lingered in the yard, enjoying the warm mid-morning sunshine. She ought to have been on the job, she thought, ferreting out facts about Hereward and Amy. She felt a stab of resentment for the Church's claims on her precious holiday. She looked round the yard. There was a fair amount going on. A couple of geldings were being loaded into the Lambourne. A farrier could be heard at work in a box on the north side and the smell of singeing hoof wafted across the yard. There was a load of hay being stacked in the barn behind the office and where the BMWs had been on Saturday, a Range Rover and an old Daimler were parked, their windows in the process of being sponged down by a boy who looked vaguely familiar. It was all orderly and business-like. A well-run enterprise.

With reluctance Theodora turned to go. She came face to face with Mrs Totteridge who was walking her sweating mare into the yard. The woman was short in inches but strong in presence. Her hands, Theodora noticed, were beautifully kept. Her jacket could have come from Oxfam, her boots, on the other hand, looked hand-made. A woman for essentials and some decoration, Theodora judged.

'George,' said Mrs Totteridge, whose voice carried well, 'come and hold Bedford for me.'

The round-headed boy who had been polishing the Daimler's windows ambled up and competently placed his hands on the rein either side of the black mare's mouth. Mrs Totteridge swung herself down from the horse's back and strode to the Range Rover. Theodora recognised the boy from her visit with the Archdeacon to the Dersinghams. He smiled round at her. 'Morning, miss. Have you had a good ride?'

'Hello. Yes, thanks. Are you going out?'

George indicated the Daimler. 'No. I brought Miss Vanessa down. She's schooling her big fellow.'

Mrs Totteridge returned holding a fistful of carrots. Theodora watched as the woman whose voice would carry across a couple of ten-acre fields, and who could bring a rowdy committee to heel by clearing her throat, murmured intimately into the mare's ear and made little clucking noises as she plied her with carrots. Theodora did the correct thing and remarked on Bedford's good looks.

'She's a good girl,' said Mrs Totteridge with restrained passion. 'Had her since she was a two-year-old.' Then, feeling perhaps that things needed to be put on a proper footing, 'Veronica Totteridge. You're staying at the Julians' I hear.'

Theodora smiled and was civil. George, who had taken the rein over Bedford's neck and had been gently rubbing her nose, seemed to have something on his mind. Finally he broke in with a rush, 'Would your goat have lost her collar, Mrs Totteridge?'

Mrs Totteridge ceased to murmur into Bedford's ear. Her eye kindled and she resumed normal service. 'Someone took it. I simply can't understand the mentality of these people. She could have been run over. What could anyone want with a collar?'

'Well, I don't know that anyone did, really. I mean, they threw it away pretty quick.'

'What are you maundering on about, George?'

'We, I, well, Leon fished it up, probably.'

'How do you mean, you probably fished it up?'

Mrs Totteridge glared at George.

'We, I, well, Leon cast into the Broad just off the reed bed over the east side, Sunday afternoon. He brought up the old goat's collar. It had her metal tag on it.'

'Where is it now?'

'That's up at the House.'

'Well, you'd better drop it in, hadn't you? If I'm out, leave it in the porch. Or probably, since you can't trust anybody anymore, you'd better put it through the letter box.' Mrs Totteridge was clearly of a mind to impute criminality to the entire population.

'Right you are,' said George equably.

Mrs Totteridge turned back to Theodora. 'So you're at the Julians'. Pretty house, isn't it? And Rosalind's such a sensible woman.' So that was all right. As far as Veronica Totteridge was concerned, Theodora was staying at the right house, riding the right sort of horse.

'I'm sorry to hear about your goat. When was her collar taken then?'

'The same night Hereward broke his neck. Friday. I keep her in the graveyard you know, at this time of year. They can't afford to put a man in and you can't get a tractor round the graves so a goat's the obvious answer. She's done quite a good job. A bit uneven in places, of course. Goats are picky. They aren't really herbivores. It's the trees they go for, given half a chance. Still, it's no way to reward a girl by nicking her collar.'

'Did she get far?'

'She trimmed up the north and east hedgerow quite nicely by the time I went up, Saturday lunchtime. Actually, if I hadn't gone to check her, Hereward might have lain there till Sunday. Nasty turn for the worshippers. Not the right frame of mind for matins. Though I suppose we need to be reminded of mortality.' Mrs Totteridge ended sententiously.

'So you found Hereward?'

'I might have missed him.' Mrs Totteridge was matter-of-fact. She could have been speaking of failing to spot an acquaintance in a crowd. 'I knew about the pit, of course, since Betty Yaxlee came a cropper in it on Friday morning. But I wasn't looking for anything in it. I'd thought there might be a bit of rope or some such in the vestry. Not a pretty sight. Dead or alive,' she added.

'Why would anyone want to kill Hereward, do you suppose?'

'I would have thought you could ask it the other way round. Why should anyone want to preserve him alive?'

'Any special reason?'

'Nasty piece of work. I know, speaking ill of the dead and all that, but really, he led poor Amy a dog's life. She was desperately lonely, poor dear.'

'She kept hens,' Theodora said inconsequentially.

'No company, hens. Not like a goat. Not intelligent.'

'I've known Buff Orpingtons whom I thought had a spark.'

'All hens give me asthma,' said Mrs Totteridge with finality.

'I thought Amy wasn't here much,' said Theodora disingenuously.

'They were both pretty absentee of late. Time was when a priest used to put it in the parish mag if he intended being out of the parish for more than twenty-four hours. What are the dying supposed to do? Hang on till he gets back? Time we had a bit of discipline in the ranks.' Mrs Totteridge banged the neck of her mare with the flat of her hand. The mare took it for affection and pushed her face into Mrs Totteridge's stomach. Mrs Totteridge staggered a bit.

'Where did he go?'

'Where indeed? Perhaps his chum over at Bestwick knows.'

'Who?'

'Topstock? Is that his name, Father Jerome Topstock? Bestwick St Clements. Just outside Diss. Stood in for Hereward at matins occasionally.' Mrs Totteridge showed signs of departing. She took her mare in hand and clicked her tongue authoritatively. 'How about sherry one evening. How about tonight? Why not? About six-ish? We're down the road on the left, Jacobean brick and a couple of montanas round the door. Pretty as a picture, we are.' She turned to go. 'Someone should have stopped Hereward, you know, before now.'

Theodora wondered what they should have stopped him doing. But Mrs Totteridge was clearly bending her mind to other things. And, after all, she'd given Theodora a name.

Reluctantly Theodora turned towards the gate to walk back to the Julians' and the interrogatory telephone. She felt again a burst of resentment against Treadwell and the Bishop. What right had they to intrude into her hard-earned holiday? It was their own indolence which had landed them with a murder which could probably be explained and might even have been prevented, if they had taken a bit more trouble. Theodora checked herself. There was no point in using energy in blaming anyone. She'd give herself one last treat and then go home and phone. She turned towards the indoor school.

Before she reached it, however, she became aware of Henry strolling across the yard. He fell in beside her and they began to converse amicably, like old acquaintances. Theodora complimented him on his orderly yard and he enquired where she had learned to ride. Then they became knowledgeable and technical about differences between national styles. Theodora was very much aware of his charm which seemed to stem not just from pleasant good looks but from a kind of inner confidence. He was relaxed, certain of himself and therefore able to allow others space and freedom. In a word, he was generous.

'You know so much about farming,' Theodora said as they were on the point of parting. 'Do you ever wish you'd farmed rather than going in for horses?'

Henry considered. 'Never,' he said finally. 'I don't think anything could give me as much pleasure as watching a horse I've bred and brought on myself performing at the top of his form.'

'Cattle aren't the same?' Theodora enquired. 'Or goats?'

Henry laughed. 'I'm very fond of that goat of Mrs Totteridge's. She's a right character. Got a will of her own.' He referred, Theodora inferred, to the goat.

'And very useful to the Church. She does a very nifty job round the graves.' Henry added.

'Father Marr should have put a flock of sheep in the churchyard in autumn. That's the traditional way,' said Theodora.

'Too sensible for the Rector,' Henry said dismissively.

'Not a man of common sense?'

Henry seemed to feel he'd gone far enough and backed off. 'Well, I suppose I've no right to say really. I didn't know him hardly at all. I'm not a churchgoer and I've no call to go visiting the Rectory. But farming now,' Henry seemed anxious to return to more familiar ground, 'isn't really possible round here. The land is still Dersingham's for the most part. And he will not let go. No, he will not.' Henry's chin jutted.

'The grazing?' Theodora prompted.

'Yes. It's not as though I can't afford to pay him market price and more. And he needs the money. That I do know. But it's pride. It's always been Dersingham land since way back when.'

Theodora thought she caught a strain of admiration in his tone. One stubborn man admiring another.

'Well,' said Henry as they reached the tiny office where he kept a telephone, 'I must go and teach my next pupil. If you've time to spare and you want to give yourself a pleasure, the Italian boy's schooling Miss Dersingham's big fellow.'

Needing no invitation, Theodora once more turned towards the school. The light was uneven in that perfect space; the corners in shadow, the long sides illuminated. Horse and rider emerged from dark to light and back again. The footfalls drummed a fast, regular pattern of coordinated trot. There was no other sound. In the centre, the dark-haired boy stood, head cocked on one side, concentrating intently on the pair as they completed circuit after circuit. He gave no verbal instruction but occasionally would gesture with his hand, like a conductor. After each such movement, the small old woman, not stiff, but poised, erect and in good rhythm with her horse, responded with minute disposition of hand, leg or body weight which the informed eye could see reflected in the horse's performance. Theodora was compelled, caught up in the intensity of the ritual as with a liturgy or a ballet. Finally, the boy spread both his arms wide. The pair moved down the centre line and halted square and dead centre. The boy's concentration lasted for a couple of seconds after the halt was achieved. Then his face broke into a huge smile. He looked up at Miss Dersingham.

'Un cavallo splendissimo.'

'And the rider?' she enquired.

'*Che bella, signorina!*'

'You teach very well, Leon. You have a future.'

'*Si.*' The boy nodded. Of his future he was perfectly confident. 'At the present time, however, it is my past that I seek,' he added.

For a moment, Miss Dersingham looked uncomprehending. 'I think you mean that you miss your family?'

'*Si.* I seek my family.'

Theodora was aware of an intimacy into which it would have been impossible to intrude. His tone, however, because of his accent, was difficult to interpret. Was it confiding, inquisitive or even threatening? Puzzled, Theodora turned away. In the distance across the yard came Henry's voice, clear and unforced, from the paddock, 'Keep the hand. *Keep* the hand. Keep the *hand*.'

* * *

'I can give you half an hour, two-thirty to three. I've got to be at the "crem" circa four.' Jerome Topstock's cultivated voice suggested that the 'crem' might be in inverted commas.

Theodora had studied the membership list of the Society of St Sylvester and used the Julians' phone and the Archdeacon's knowledge thereafter. There were three St Sylvester's men in the Diocese of Norwich beside Hereward. Two were in the neighbourhood of Walsingham. One of these two, when checked with the Archdeacon, proved to be dead. The other was on holiday in Scotland, address unknown. That left the third, who turned out to be Mrs Totteridge's Father Topstock. The Membership List revealed he'd been in his present parish for six years, was unmarried, had written a book, *The Railways of Norfolk, 1890 to 1940*, published by Jarrolds, and was, in addition to being Vicar of St Clements Bestwick, chaplain to the Sisters of St Sylvester, East Soken, near Diss. Theodora was about to shut the list when her eye lit upon the final sentence in the entry. It ran, Archivist, St Sylvester, 1980 to 84. So, thought Theodora, he would know. The question was, would he tell?

Theodora had spread out the Ordnance Survey and fended off Tobias long enough to make out a route. Then she had taken bread and cheese and coffee and started across Norfolk, giving, as she drove, some thought to the strategy best suited to extracting information from this Anglican priest in the Catholic wing.

It was Theodora's habit to visit churches before tackling incumbents. The building often revealed the man. Faint dot-matrix notices from ill-understood PCWs signalled one approach to parochial administration, handwritten messages in washed-out green biro about where to find the church building's keys another. Complicated timetables of services, juggling of ASBs with 1662s spread over five venues usually indicated that the first enquiry should be a suitably sympathetic one about 'how things were in the parishes'. Clearly no one person could get round five parishes, control five PCCs, prop up the fabric of five buildings, look to a couple of church school governing bodies, visit, bury and comfort the sick, dead and bereaved, let alone baptise, prepare for confirmation and marry five sets of parishioners and at the same time keep up a life of prayer. The problems which faced the Church now were not, Theodora thought, so very different from those which had faced those young priests for whom the Reverend Thomas Henry Newcome had founded St Sylvester's in the 1860s.

This time, however, she was so late that she could not reconnoitre first. The vicarage, when she found it, was of grey brick in the middle of a flat field, far from the village and out of sight of the church. Everything in the view was well spread out. There was a feeling of an immense canvas which the artist had been unsure how to fill. As though trying to use up a bit of space, the garage (for a single car) was situated a hundred yards from the house, up a separate track. There was no garden; the harsh fen grasses ended in a coarse frill flapping against the walls of the gaunt house. Even in August it looked cold. There were no trees and the nearest defining hedge was a quarter of a mile away, beyond a desert of sugar beet, its squat green leaves hugging the soil as though unwilling to risk rising up into the wide air.

What sort of character would have sustained this setting for six years, Theodora wondered, as she parked the car in the hedgerow and lifted the wicket gate six inches in order to swing it open. The way to the front door was of long, unevenly sunken slabs of concrete so that the path was little more than a series of stepping stones. She glanced at her watch: twenty minutes past two. On the door was a notice in faded green biro: 'Baptisms and Marriages, Tuesdays 6.30 to 7 p.m. only. Church hall bookings: see Mrs Crane, the Cottage, the Loke, Bestwick.' How many did he pull in on a Sunday, she wondered, given such meagre treatment. Below this information was drawn a thin wavy arrow and the word 'Entrance'. Theodora circled the house in the direction of the arrow and came round to the back door. It was open and through it came the sound of a cello. On a bentwood kitchen chair of giant proportions was a very large man in a soutane, his sleeves rolled up, his enormous hands cradling the instrument and his head bent forward to listen. His immense sandalled feet, on which black clerical socks could be seen, were planted far apart, holding down, as it seemed, the stone-flagged floor. So that was how he kept sane. Theodora waited. He finished his passage and put the bow on the table beside him. Theodora said nothing. She had always found it easy to wait, to say nothing, to live in the silence of the moment. Gradually the memory of the music receded from the large, cold kitchen; the tall man stood up and smiled. He was completely bald, but not shinily so, rather with a soft downy finish over his domed head. His eyes were small, deep grey, and snapped at her from behind round steel-framed glasses.

'It seems a pity to interrupt,' Theodora said.

'It always does with music. But at some point one has to stop and resort to speech.' There was doubt and regret in his tone. Theodora warmed to him.

'You sound,' Theodora was hesitant, not wanting to patronise, 'accomplished'.

'I have the leisure to practise.'

Not five parishes then.

'Tea?' He turned as naturally as any other cleric to the small domestic hospitality. He wasn't, however, going to help her in any other way.

She took the cup of tea-bag Indian and allowed him to settle himself at the large deal table covered with music scores. He leaned back in his ample chair, the back of which rose up behind him, framing him like a mandorca. He did no more than raise an eyebrow.

Truth is the rock, when in doubt, Theodora told herself. 'I've been asked by the Bishop to find out something about the background of Hereward Marr and his wife,' she tried, as an opener.

Father Topstock crossed himself.

'He was an associate of the Society of St Sylvester and you, I think, were the archivist of the Society for a time.'

He nodded, curtly. 'One, what sort of things does the Bishop want to know?' he asked. 'Two, why does he want to know them? Three, why doesn't he ask me himself or set his Archdeacon on. I was at his recent garden party and I have actually shaken his hand. I am not completely unknown to him, after all.'

Fleetingly Theodora wondered whether the ironic tone was further evidence that the Bishop was generally thought not to know his own clergy. 'The Bishop didn't specify in detail what he wanted to know, but I imagine he fears that Father Marr was killed because of something in his unknown past which may not be entirely creditable to the church. He asked me because I'm serving a curacy at St Sylvester's Betterhouse. I know Gilbert Racy and I happen to be on holiday in Hereward's parish.' She felt this was quite enough without mentioning her acquaintance with Amy.

'Oh ho. A deaconess.'

Theodora waited to see which way it would go.

'I don't approve of them,' he stated.

This was no place for a theological argument and it was essential she get on terms. 'I don't suppose we'll come to anything, would you say?' she asked with restrained politeness.

'I'm not threatened,' he said defensively. 'I quite like women actually, but not at the altar.'

Really, how fatuous this all was. There was a place for tradition but it was not here. Topstock's little grey eyes snapped through his steel frames under the great downy dome. Theodora was struck anew by how much a physical presence determined what could and could not be said.

But she was determined to resist his intimidation. 'I'm not allowed an altar,' she said, registering, to her annoyance, the note of desperation in her voice.

'But I bet you want one,' he said, as though clinching an argument.

'We don't always get what we want,' she answered with clipped control, 'and learning to deal with that is just as much a part of the Christian life as any other experience.'

'That's another reason I don't want women priested. They'll take the moral high ground all the time. We shall feel such heels.'

Theodora smiled with genuine pleasure at his honesty. 'Yes. I can see it might be tiresome for you. Did Hereward feel as you do?'

'Did you say your name was Braithwaite?'

'Yes.'

'Nicholas was . . . ?'

'. . . Was my father. Canon Hugh is my great uncle.'

'Yes. I see.'

'It makes a difference?'

'I used to hear your father preach when I was at Oxford. I admired him greatly. In fact, I think I owe my vocation to him.'

So tradition could work both ways. Theodora prayed her gratitude.

'I was so very sorry to hear of his early death.' The eyes looked straight at her, empty, now, of all slyness, and full, she thought, of real sympathy. Since he had been genuine and generous Theodora would not hold back.

'I miss him, all the time, I think, in one way or another.'

Topstock stirred a lot of sugar into his tea and resumed. 'Hereward then. Why?'

'I knew his wife, Amy. She was in dire straits. I think he may have been responsible for her unhappiness. People keep telling me he should have stopped. If that's at all true, I'd like to help to get things straight. "Thy household the church", you know. We ought to run things properly and see if we can't do things better in future.'

'Yes. I see. You sound very like Nicholas.'

Theodora was near to tears. He mustn't keep on like this, she felt. She wasn't prepared. 'It's his motives,' she said, gathering her resources. 'I can't see why. How. I don't know enough of his background, the causal chain.' She gazed at him, waiting.

Topstock sighed. 'His father,' he began — and Theodora knew she was home and dry — 'was a regular army officer. He badly wanted an army son. Instead he had Hereward, who was not by any means army. He wasn't even sound. One leg was a bit shorter than the other, I think. The family came from somewhere in the West Country. Father made life very unpleasant for Hereward.' He paused, 'And "those to whom evil is done . . ."'

'"Do evil in return."'

'Quite so. The father shot himself one afternoon after having shot his wife. Hereward was about fifteen at the time.'

'And his vocation?'

'Was fostered by Matthew Jacob.'

Theodora caught at the name. 'Didn't he have a hand in Gilbert Racy's conversion?'

Topstock paused for a moment and then said, 'I think he was responsible for a good many of the Society's priests. And . . .'

Theodora took his meaning, '. . . sometimes he got it right and sometimes not?'

'I think that would be fair,' said the archivist. 'Of course I'm not being heretical here. God can use any of us, any one at all. It's just that the vocation to the priesthood . . . we need to be very prayerful about it. It is so very important.'

'Quite so.' Theodora was generous enough to have no irony at all in her tone. 'Anyway, he *was* priested?'

'Oh yes. The Bishop of Oxford did him, I seem to remember. In terms of work it was a real way out for Hereward from his appalling home background. It gave him everything and he may have been genuinely intending good. To repair the balance.'

Theodora understood this. 'But?'

'Have you read him on the sacrament of penance?'

'Yes. No. Well I know the article he wrote for the Society's Quarterly. I didn't actually read it,' she confessed.

'You'd better. The causality you're looking for is there.' Father Topstock glanced at his watch, wound his hands round his mug and leaned forward. He spoke rapidly, as a man due at the crematorium in half an hour. 'I don't honestly know the details. Until you told me about Amy, I didn't guess, that either.' He paused. 'Please believe me.' He wanted her absolution.

Theodora, no priest, gave it readily, 'I'm sure. Not many people did know. Though of course Gilbert Racy did.'

'Yes, I suppose that's true'. Topstock clearly didn't know what to make of that.

Theodora changed tack. 'Marr was often absent from the parish. Can you think why that should be, or where he went?'

'He had a hobby,' Topstock said slowly.

'Genealogy?' Theodora enquired.

'You knew?'

'I visited the Rectory. The books open on the library floor were mostly genealogical.'

'He was obsessed with heredity and entitlement. It could look like snobbery in conversation, but if you take it together with his family background and his interest in penance, it might look more like coming to terms with an inherited stain.'

'So his absences?'

'I'd see if the Royal College of Heralds remembers him.' Father Topstock looked up from his mug and concentrated his gaze fully on Theodora. 'Families can sustain or suffocate. You were very lucky.'

'Oh, I know, I know,' Theodora answered with fervour untroubled now by his allusion to her own past. 'I don't judge him. I just feel the church should take reasonable precautions.'

Topstock seemed to think he'd done his duty. He relaxed his grip on the mug, rolled his sleeves down, pushed his chair back.

Theodora rose. 'I'm very grateful.'

The little grey eyes glinted again. 'God bless. Safe journey. Read the article.'

CHAPTER TEN: INSPECTOR SPRUCE

Spruce looked up. 'What time was this?'

'Quarter to eleven,' the Reverend Pat Tilley answered.

'You're sure about that?'

'Sure as eggs is eggs,' she answered in her unashamedly yokel voice.

'What were you doing there?'

'I'd been to have a bun and a squint at Mrs Y's telly, or, to put it another way, Inspector, doing a pastoral visit to a sick member of the congregation.'

Spruce looked at her statement. 'On Friday evening you were passing the Rectory at a quarter to twelve midnight by the chime of the church clock. You thought you saw a figure entering the front door of the Rectory.'

'I didn't *think*, I *saw*. It was full moon, Inspector,' Miss Tilley rounded her eyes to help the Inspector with this concept. 'There was enough light from the moon and from the light in the house to see a figure.'

'What did it look like, this figure?'

'I've told you. It looked tall but I only saw it for a moment.'

'Who let it in?'

Miss Tilley thought for a moment. 'I don't think anyone let it in, I'd guess the door was open or it had a key.'

'Did you see any signs of anyone else there?'

'How do you mean?'

'Were there any cars or bicycles?'

'Not that I could see.'

'Could you identify the figure you saw going in?'

'I just said, it looked to me at first as though it was a woman, then just something made me think it might be a man.'

'What made you think that, Miss Tilley?' said Spruce patiently.

'The way he moved, his shape, perhaps.' Miss Tilley was disappointed with herself. She never liked to be less than definite. But truth compelled.

'So you couldn't go as far as saying who it might have been calling on the Rector at that late hour?'

'If I were you I'd make a list of tall men and women in the village with bad characters and check their alibis,' advised Miss Tilley judiciously, one professional to another.

'What did you do after you'd observed the figure?' asked Spruce patiently.

'I went on my way, wondering.'

'Where?'

'Home. Natch.'

'You didn't think it was odd that someone should call on the Rector that late at night?'

'We clergy,' said the Reverend Pat Tilley grandly, 'get called on and out at all sorts of odd times. Only safe on the loo and not always then.'

'And you live?'

Miss Tilley gestured with her index finger pointing upwards to the classroom ceiling. 'Here, over the shop. Well, in the schoolhouse flat, actually. I do point five for Mrs Martineu. Bottom juniors at the mo.'

'You noticed nothing else out of the way then, or at any other time?'

'Don't think so. Depends, of course, what you mean by odd. There were one or two cows round the place.'

'Cows?'

'They live, or they're supposed to live, in the paddock between the Rectory and the House, but the fencing needs seeing to, so they tend to wander round the Rectory when they want. They don't do any harm. It's not as though there was a garden to ruin.'

'No. Well. Anything else out of the way that might help us?'

'It depends what you mean by out of the way. I mean, Hereward was odd.'

'How did it manifest itself?'

'Digging up the church heating isn't normal.'

'Why did he do that?'

'His tale was that it wasn't working properly. The PCC didn't believe him. They wanted to get in the diocesan surveyor to have a look at it before they shelled out for repairs. Hereward wouldn't have that for some reason, so he took his little spade and started himself.'

Spruce sighed. He'd heard the story from three other people questioned in the village. It didn't seem to lead anywhere. 'The school is about a quarter of a mile from the Rectory. You didn't see anything else on your return home?'

'Not a sausage.'

In his spare time Spruce climbed rocks in Wales and Scotland. He felt much the same sensation now as he searched around for a fresh foothold. 'How well did you know Mr and Mrs Marr, Miss Tilley?'

'Well, he wasn't the chummy sort. I mean we're all in the same boat.' Miss Tilley touched her clerical collar. 'And I've been in the parish longer than he has. But he wasn't one for being matey, or even civil. Rather coughed his orders out. I mean, as I told Dick Treadwell, we're supposed to be colleagues. He seemed to think I might be the tea lady.'

'How about Mrs Marr?'

'She kept in the background rather. Didn't have many friends.'

'Was anyone in the village close to her?'

'She knew the Totteridges. But then who doesn't? She took up riding at one point, but that didn't come to anything. She wasn't sporty. I thought at first she was going to lend a hand. Do a bit of youth work, take the tots for junior church, you know the sort of thing.'

Spruce nodded his best ingratiating nod. 'But?' he prompted her.

'In fact she backed off that too. The most she ever did was a bit of sick visiting. She helped a lot when Ted Yaxlee was dying. I'll give her that.'

Spruce consulted his list, failing to make any sort of connection and asked, not for the first time in the enquiry, 'Which Yaxlee would that be?'

'Betty's son. She of the hole.'

'The hole?'

'Hereward's folly, his church hole. She fell in it Friday lunchtime, yes?'

Spruce realised he was getting tired. 'Oh, yes.'

'Well, her son, Ted, George's dad, died of cancer of the bowel. Nasty. This time last year. He was Dersingham's factotum, if you get me. Hereward didn't, naturally, do any of the hard, if you see what I mean. The sick need to be able to depend on people visiting when they say they will and that wouldn't have suited Hereward at all. Ted wasn't that churchy' — the Deaconess condescended to Spruce — '"committed", Inspector, in our lingo. But he came more than he might have and he'd done a bit with the bells in his heyday. For the beer, I expect. Liked his tipple. What I mean is, he'd a right to a bit of visiting when he was dying.'

Spruce put the conversation back on the rails. 'But Mrs Marr did visit Yaxlee.'

'Yes, regularly. And she was good at it. Professional. Knew what to say. How to make him laugh. Took him bits of things. He liked puzzles. He was mechanical. Rubik's cubes and Chinese things. Yes. It's a shame about poor old Amy.'

'How "shame"?'

'Well, I suppose she's a gonner, yes?'

'Why should you suppose that?'

'The car in the Broad.'

'We don't know that she was drowned,' said Spruce evenly. And indeed it was true. Everyone was assuming she had been. But they'd had men dragging those stinking waters for twenty-four hours and they'd come up with nothing. Spruce sighed. 'And on Saturday afternoon when the car went into the Broad, where were you, Miss Tilley?'

'Norwich. Bishop's bunfight. Then I stopped off to do a bit of shopping, cash in Betty Y's prescription et cetera. I got back half-six.'

That seemed to be that then. 'Thank you very much, Miss Tilley. We may have to be in touch again. Meanwhile, if there's anything, anything at all, you think we ought to know, you . . .'

'. . . Know where to find you. Right. Cheerio for now, Inspector. Good hunting.'

Spruce leaned back in his chair. It had been a tiring day, largely because it had been so unproductive. The Chief Inspector had rung. The Chief Constable, for God's sake, had rung, doubtless spurred by the Dersingham connection. The many journalists, who had sprung up from nowhere, he'd left to his sergeant. Odd how a priest's death was news. Any other old drunk would have got a corner on the fourth page.

He raised his gaze to the middle distance and caught the red button eye of the dinosaur squatting on the check tablecloth beside the vase of dahlias. Round the wall of the classroom romped and danced a frieze of tyrannosauruses, megalosauruses and brontosauruses, in primary colours. The drawing was vigorous, the vegetation through which they moved vividly rendered. Something had touched the imaginations of the young artists. Perhaps they felt pity and affection for the animals moving through a world by which they were doomed to be destroyed. Climate, was it, change of vegetation or some meteorite activity which ended them? The class was exploring prehistory. No bad way, Spruce reflected, to prepare them for life in the modern, dangerous world.

It had seemed a good idea to set up his incident room in the local primary school. It was holiday time, the building was centrally placed in the village; it had a phone, a sink and a photocopier. The cleaner, Mrs Marge Yaxlee, was, when contacted by the LEA, compliant, and even, by Norfolk standards, helpful. Spruce was surprised, therefore, by the degree of nostalgia which disturbed, even afflicted him. The too-small chairs, the miniature tables, the intimate cherished objects temporarily abandoned by teachers and pupils, as though awaiting term-time and contact with their owners to stop them seeming ridiculous and warm them once again into significance, intruded upon his concentration. He felt the ghost of his earlier life round him. If he closed his eyes, he was back in his own pupillage.

He got up and wandered round the room. It had been a single hall. Now it was divided by a folding partition into two classrooms. All the plastic tranklements of modern primary education could not disguise the fact that the room was basically a solid Victorian construction, built to last. Boy-proof, Spruce thought, as he felt the solidity of the place about him; the product of very different values from the ones currently holding sway in education. On the roof beam, stretching above him across the whole width of the room, was carved and gilded the minatory text, 'God's eye seeth all'. Well, thought Spruce, recalling his Methodist boyhood, true enough, and I wish I could do the same right now.

He stopped in his perambulation and his gaze fell on the table by the window (set too high for children to see out of), on which was laid out a display of local history material. There were photographs of the village street at the turn of the century, some cobblers' tools, two army cap badges and a photograph of a cricket team about 1930. The gentlemen, presumably Dersinghams, were easily distinguishable from the village players. At the far end of the display was the school log-book. Spruce, turning the pages idly, found an entry for a Monday in February 1877: three pupils had been beaten for disorderly behaviour in church the previous Sunday. No wonder the C of E had not endeared itself to the working classes, Spruce reflected. What, here in St Benet Oldfield, had it ever done for them? What, for that matter, did it do for them now? Except, to be fair, provide education — well — schooling, at least of a sort.

Spruce turned back to his own table. This was just indulgent. He had a murdered priest on his hands, a missing wife, and a drowned car. No motives, no background, just a picture with nothing but foreground and a wide empty Norfolk sky behind it. He riffled through the statements he'd taken so far. The questions had, for the most part, been slanted to the factual points about where people were on Friday night and Saturday afternoon.

On Friday night Lord Dersingham had been playing patience. This had come, very firmly, from Miss Vanessa, while she herself had been at her tapestry. They had seen and heard nothing unusual. Dersingham had added that he'd had his whisky at ten-thirty and gone up half an hour later. On Saturday, early afternoon, he'd gone into the city to get his watch repaired and returned about five o'clock. The watchmaker confirmed he'd been with him at two. The boy manservant, George Yaxlee, had said he'd gone to the stable to meet Leon, the Italian boy, at nine on Friday night; they had stayed together, first at the stable, then at the darts final at the Dersingham Arms until ten-thirty. Then they'd returned to the stable and George had got back to the House about midnight. He'd seen nothing out of the way. On Saturday, he'd cleaned the silver in the morning, done a bit round the House and visited his gran in the afternoon, returning at 3 p.m. The Totteridges asserted that they had read till eleven on Friday and then gone to bed. On Saturday Mrs Totteridge had ridden in the morning and then at lunchtime had checked her goat with the attendant events from which the whole enquiry had followed. She had not, she said, seen anything in the least suspicious other, of course, than the body of the Rector. Mr Totteridge had spent the day in the garden until five p.m. and then apparently unperturbed, they had driven out to dine with friends in Norwich. Nothing had struck him as out of the ordinary apart of course from his wife's news about the Rector, communicated to him around tea-time. They seemed, Spruce thought, to be extremely laid back about the whole affair. However that didn't make them guilty of murder. Henry Yaxlee said that on Friday night he'd done the accounts till quite late, made a round of the stables about eleven-thirty and gone to bed soon after. On Saturday, he had been tied up all day in the stable, but had taken a walk round the Broad over the lunch hour. He's seen nothing out of the way. Amongst the villagers, the division on Friday night was between the men, who had been in the pub and could vouch for each other, and the wives, who had been watching telly at home and couldn't, but who seemed knowledgeable, when pressed, about a number of ITV programmes. On Saturday afternoon, most of the men had gone to watch City at home, most of the women had taken to the washing machine. So much, thought Spruce, for the cultural life of a Norfolk village at the end of the twentieth century.

On Friday night, therefore, Miss Tilley's was the only information which seemed to lead anywhere. Was she reliable? And if so, who had she seen? The other bit of information came from the Bishop's female Deacon, what was her name? Spruce ran his eye down his list. Braithwaite, the Reverend T.E.O. She'd seen, she averred, Amy, or anyway her car, coming down the Julians' drive at about ten-thirty on Friday night. What had the car gone on to? And, for that matter, where had it come from? Had it, at any point, gone to the churchyard?

The scene of the crime had produced little. The good weather had left the ground hard. There were no identifiable footprints. The church was used by a fair number of people towards the end of any week. Village help of the Yaxlee variety came to do the flowers and clean the floor. The odd, persistent tourist might have come and, now he came to think of it, where were animal footprints, presumably of the goat, or, in the light of Miss Tilley's remarks, the cattle. The path from the back of the Rectory to the church, though legally a public bridle path, was in fact almost a private drive used by the Rector and occasionally by riders cutting across to the Broad. Normal visitors to the church would come by the main road.

What made it all so difficult was that, though practically no one had had a good word to say for Hereward, no one could or would pin down that dislike into a form which could prime a hatred violent enough to kill him. The police research, so far, had elicited little more than what was in *Crockford.* They had got his birth certificate, which confirmed he was the only son of Sydney Marriot Marr, Major, late of the Royal Artillery, and Helen Marie Armitage. The Army List told him the father was dead, the Registrar General that his wife was. The Emmanuel College list gave him minimal information about matriculation and tripos results. But he had received a fax from the Bishop of the Diocese of Europe. Wearily Spruce picked it up and glanced at it again. It asserted that Hereward had held cures in Malta and Italy and the Bishop 'had every confidence in his ability fully to discharge the duties of Rector of St Benet Oldfield. He would be happy to answer further questions, etc.' Spruce felt despair enter his soul. About Amy he had drawn a complete blank. There were no marriage lines and no birth certificate to be had from public records. Where had she come from? Could she have been born abroad, he wondered? Was she capable, physically or mentally, of killing Hereward? He had absolutely no sense of the woman, least of all where she was now. Dead or alive? Guilty or innocent? Spruce could not help feeling that if he knew more about Hereward and Amy, he would have more of a grip on the case. Why was the church so ignorant of her own men and women? His eye lit again upon the dinosaur. Not unlike Anglican bishops, he felt, impressive enough in bulk but with tiny, tiny heads.

Spruce allowed his mind to run back over the meeting with the Bishop, Archdeacon and Miss Braithwaite. Miss Braithwaite was clearly a different kettle of fish from the other Deaconess he'd met, Miss Tilley. They came, then, in all shapes and sizes these female deacons, like policemen. Miss Braithwaite had picked up the gap in Hereward's curriculum vitae fast enough. She'd volunteered the information about Amy's marital relationships. And she'd mentioned the sighting of Amy on Friday night and Saturday morning. But now he came to consider it, she'd had an air of knowing more than she'd let on throughout the proceedings. Would this be because she had something to hide, he wondered, or was she inhibited by her clerical top brass. The whole meeting had struck him as quite remarkably hierarchical. She'd been almost too self-effacing, he thought. Her manner, though polite, had a glacial quality. Not a very comfortable personality. She'd been reserved in a way which suggested that she might be strong-willed but was making an effort to hide it or keep it in check. Was she used to being more intelligent than those she dealt with and it being inappropriate to show it? Well, if the norm in the Church was the Bishop and Miss Tilley, you could see she'd have a fair amount of concealing to do.

From the next room came the sound of his sergeant, fresh from his success on a computer course, tirelessly cross-referencing statements. Spruce reached for the phone. It was 6 p.m. He might just catch her.

'Miss Braithwaite? Inspector Spruce here. Would you be available at all tomorrow? Any time at your convenience. Well, that's very kind of you. That would be a most welcome break. One o'clock then.'

CHAPTER ELEVEN: THE TOTTERIDGES

Alan Totteridge balanced the Siamese cat carefully in both hands and elevated her like the host. He gazed deeply into her eyes and said, 'Your first visit, to Oldfield, is it?'

Theodora surmised that the question was addressed to her. 'More or less. I came here once as a child. I've really no memory of the place.'

'Ah,' said Alan, lowering the cat to his lap and stroking her head with a single large finger. 'My people have always been here. We're slightly older than the present Dersinghams. But not as greedy, so not as successful.' He looked immensely pleased at his family's lack of success and smiled knowingly into the cat's eyes. 'There was a Totteridge with Harold at Hastings.' He gazed at the ceiling above the cat's head.

Theodora leaned back in her chair and glanced about her. Her own taste was austere. In old houses she preferred old furniture of a single period and the Totteridges clearly thought the same. Here three Jacobean cottages had been knocked into one, although, understandably the furniture was a little younger. There was a display of early eighteenth-century Chinese porcelain of great excellence across two walls and Mrs Totteridge's neat figure was framed by swirling blue dragons chasing their tails round dramatic mountain ranges.

Theodora thought back to the dilapidated drawing room of the Dersinghams. Worldly success was relative.

Veronica Totteridge bent forward to replenish their sherry glasses. Her rings sparkled, her deep-red silk shirt glowed in the evening sunlight which slanted through the open window. The garden beyond had been knowledgeably cultivated. The smell of Nicotianas and musk rose hung in the air. After her mental exertions across country with Father Topstock, Theodora gave herself up to the pleasure of being entertained.

'You could hardly call the Dersinghams successful,' Veronica's powerful voice filled the room. 'And I'm not sure about greedy. They hang on but it's all a bit desperate.'

Alan's long square head, with its thatch of silvery gold hair, failed to turn towards his wife. He specialised, it seemed, in not responding to the emotions of others, preferring to mark time until he could, with maximum effect, present his own. Theodora speculated on the nature of the relationship between the two of them. He was perhaps fifteen years older than she, as relaxed, in a deliberate sort of way, as she was energetic. She judged them to be in a total accord with each other. They seemed set on dissecting the Dersinghams. Theodora had no objection. She felt the more she knew about them, the more she might come across a link with Hereward.

'The present lot,' said Alan, gazing deeply into his cat's eyes again, 'are only married in. The male line gave out in the early eighteenth century. Viola Dersingham married Leonard Markham about 1720. He was the second son of the Earl of Cumbermound. The second creation is via Walpole in 1740, to whom of course they truckled. So really the present lot aren't Dersinghams at all.'

'You don't think females can pass on a proper inheritance?' said Theodora.

'The Salic Law,' murmured Mrs Totteridge.

'Very un-English piece of law that,' said Alan with deliberation.

'Not that any sort of law would help the present lot. They can't even raise a daughter between them, let alone a son,' Mrs Totteridge said with finality.

'There are no children, then, either illegitimate or legitimate?' Theodora asked.

There was a pause. Theodora wondered how far Alan's delight in displaying historical knowledge to his cat would outweigh the impropriety of gossiping to strangers. The cat blinked and Alan continued. 'So they say. So they say. But of course there are always the soldiery.'

Theodora wondered whether he had any particular soldiery in mind or whether this was a general term of his to designate opportunities for extra-marital matings.

'Sherry,' said Mrs Totteridge forcefully.

Theodora managed to smile her thanks without taking either her eye or her attention from Alan. She concentrated all her considerable powers on him, willing him to continue. But Veronica cut in. 'The girls have always had more about them than the boys. They'd have done better to route the inheritance that way.'

'"Primogeniture and due of birth",' said Alan with relish.

Theodora ventured to prompt him, 'Miss Dersingham — the present one — I noticed when I visited with the Archdeacon the other evening the tapestry she's doing. It's a set of her family's arms taken from the hatchment in the chapel, I think. But they're set inside a lozenge and shown without the crest . . .'

Glancing up, Alan for the first time looked her in the eye, forgetting himself so far as to respond, 'Is that so? How very interesting.'

Veronica broke into the conversation with all the finesse of a really determined rider on a poor jumper approaching a tricky fence. 'Imagine seventy years of life with Louis. And before that the old horror of a Baron. No wonder she's a bit batty, poor dear. Riding's her only interest as far as I can see.' Mrs Totteridge went on with a fine contempt. 'Then it's all that dressage. Whoever wants a horse to piaffe, anyway? It's all so constricted.'

Like their world, Theodora reflected.

'We're a very complete village here, you know,' Alan seemed to have bowed to his wife's wish to turn the conversation. 'Dersingham has kept it that way and for all his faults I like it. We have a pub, a shop, a great House, a church, a school and a doctor. Human life is perfectly catered for. We even have—' he lowered his eyes to his cat in modesty — 'If I may say so, a chronicler of our history in myself.'

Mrs Totteridge gazed admiringly at her husband. 'He was a lawyer, you know,' she said intimately to Theodora, as though Alan were not present or could not hear them. 'I always think they make the best historians, don't you?'

Theodora was caught off-guard. The idea of Mrs Totteridge having enough scholarly experience to make this judgement shook her. 'Yes, indeed,' she murmured. 'Your model village can't be very common nowadays.'

'Norfolk is only just ceasing to be remote,' Alan said with pride. 'There are one or two of us still left.'

'What would happen if the Dersingham family died out?' Theodora asked.

'We should get a yuppy from London who'd farm us properly,' said Veronica. 'Main drains, arable and a yachting marina.'

'Reason enough to find an heir to prevent that,' said Theodora.

'Well, of course, Dersingham could have gone for a modified development. Not the theme park heritage nonsense, but there was no point in not letting Henry have his bits of grazing. Horses are a reality after all. There's nothing bogus about them.' Mrs Totteridge knew what she was talking about.

'Why wouldn't he allow Henry to expand?' Theodora enquired.

'Oh they're old enemies. They are the family, of course, but they don't pay their livery bills. Henry, on the whole, has prospered by his own efforts. Dersingham has never really done anything. And Henry, well, he's not deferential. I think he feels the Dersinghams have had their time and he doesn't bother to hide that. Dersingham thinks of Henry as a villager, which in a sense he is. But he was educated at the local grammar school and did his national service in the cavalry. He's been abroad through his horse dealing and he's comfortable with all sorts of people. He didn't marry but it wasn't for want of opportunity.'

Theodora felt an immense weariness. 'I've spent the afternoon with a priest who feels women shouldn't have altars because we might make men feel morally inferior,' she said. 'It strikes me that you seem to have a similar problem here: a village failing because the only heirs can't inherit because they're female and the only vigorous successors are thwarted as upstarts. Frustration all round.'

'So you went to see Jerome Topstock,' said Mrs Totteridge with rekindled interest. 'They were big laymen, the Topstocks, in the fens when I was a girl.'

'It's odd, isn't it,' Theodora remarked, 'this division into Church families and non-Church. It seems to cut across class boundaries. Some families just are and some are not.'

Mrs Totteridge nodded. 'And those who aren't can't really understand why those who are, are.'

'I sometimes feel that the real Church has gone underground,' said Theodora. 'I know whole networks of families in the evangelical tradition who pass guests on to each other from abroad. Foster children, impecunious students, the disabled. Quite genuinely not counting the cost. And then in the Catholic wing, too, much the same happens. Not so much, I think, amongst the laity but the clergy form brotherhoods which seem to act as support systems as well as pressure groups within the church politics.'

'Like the St Sylvester men,' Alan Totteridge contributed judiciously. Theodora nodded. As a churchman and historian he clearly knew about Catholic societies. But had that system worked for Hereward, she wondered? What had it given him and what had he contributed? And had Amy had any share of its support, apart from when things got really bad and she'd ended up in London? 'What was wrong with

Hereward?' she asked, determinedly, fixing Alan Totteridge's evasive eye.

But it was Veronica who answered. 'He seemed to think that being a priest didn't just set him apart from everyone else but above them too. Even in the village where there's a good deal of that, it's just not on as a general stance any more. Taking and giving nothing back. He used his high churchmanship to exclude and humiliate, to make people feel guilty, almost to punish them. At times he seemed to ape the Dersinghams — he had the same sort of voice and the same sort of mannerisms. And he seemed to think that he could be curt and rude and damned patronising, and that it didn't matter. That there were no consequences or aftermath. But of course there always is, isn't there? Some consequence, I mean?' She appealed half anxiously to Theodora as though, having ventured down paths she did not normally travel, Theodora would be her guide.

Theodora concurred. 'Yes. There's always a consequence. We may not notice it but we never get away with it.' Though it doesn't always have the result of death, Theodora thought privately. But if people as balanced and sane as the Totteridges felt so strongly about him as this, perhaps it wasn't too difficult to think someone else less balanced might have felt he deserved to die. She could see that in a society as narrow as it was possible still to be, where the relationships, for large numbers of its members, consisted simply of giving and receiving orders, of looking up or looking down, someone who overstepped the mark, at a time when that pattern was being questioned, might conceivably land up with his neck broken. Theodora sighed. The ancient connection between Church and state was bumping towards its end. Marrs and Dersinghams together would kill it. 'What about Amy?' she asked, resolved to explore every avenue the Totteridge's local knowledge might provide. 'Do you know where she came from?'

Mrs Totteridge shrugged. 'I don't know anything about her family. She never spoke of them. But she did tell me once that she'd been a nurse before she met Hereward. I somehow assumed she might have nursed him in hospital.'

Theodora tensed. If Amy had been a nurse, would that have given her enough knowledge of anatomy to kill her husband? And could that fact have been known to Gilbert? The thought was appalling.

'There were rumours of an heir,' Alan said suddenly.

Theodora almost groaned. She didn't want there to be an heir. The thought of anyone taking on the mantle of Dersingham, keeping the whole unhealthy set-up going depressed her inordinately. As far as she was concerned if there was an heir it would be best if he was left to whatever obscurity he had sunk.

Once started, however, Alan continued. Was he, Theodora wondered, moved, at least partly, by his feeling of the superiority of his family to the Dersinghams? Certainly he seemed propelled by something.

'It was just after the war, after Leopold had hanged himself. I was newly articled in my uncle's firm. We had, indeed *have,* chambers in the close. The old Baron sent a note to my uncle to say he wanted to change his will. Usually, of course, Uncle Martin went to Dersingham but on this occasion Dersingham came in person. I suppose he may not have wanted the rest of the family to know or guess the reason for his visit. I don't know what the changes were but I was in the outer office when Dersingham was being shown out, and I saw Uncle Martin's face. He wasn't indiscreet but I was family. "For generations," he said, "there've been too few Dersinghams. Now it looks as though there's one too many."'

'Who would that have been?' Theodora enquired.

'To be a legitimate heir, it would have to have been a son of Leopold or Louis, born after a legal marriage. There's no question of the barony going down through a woman.' Alan was definite. 'The entail was upon the eldest son and the property goes with the title.'

'How about ages?' Theodora was suddenly alert.

'In 1947 Louis would have been twenty and Leopold of course died in 1942 at eighteen. There were two years between them.' Alan the historian liked a dating problem.

'And the mother?' Veronica enquired.

'Who knows?' said Alan.

'What happened?' his wife pursued.

'Nothing. The old Baron saw my uncle in the spring of '46. In '47, just before he died, he changed his will again, ordered previous wills to be destroyed and the family was left with the inheritance as we know it now.'

Theodora had partly lost interest. 'I don't see how this could bring about Hereward's murder,' she said wearily.

'Hereward knew about the heir,' said Mrs Totteridge unexpectedly.

Theodora sat up. It was the first breakthrough. The first time anything like a motive had hoved into view. 'How do you know?'

'Amy told me.'

Theodora prompted her to continue, 'And?'

'We were doing the flowers in St Benet one Friday evening last year. It was dark, early February time, Epiphany. Amy was deeply unhappy. She wanted children, I know. We were going out through the Dersingham chapel door. I don't know if you know the Dersingham chapel?'

Theodora nodded.

'Well, you'll know there are rather a lot of children there, one way or another, sculptured or buried. Amy stopped beside the tablet of the eldest son of the old Baron, the young Leopold — the one who hanged himself before the war. Amy said, "I sometimes sympathise with Dersingham and Vanessa. I think both in their ways wanted children." I made some sort of banal remark, you know, the way one does when people start confiding and you wish they wouldn't because it does no good and they only resent you afterwards.'

'And then?' Theodora pursued.

'Well, then she said, rather low so I didn't at first take it on board, "Hereward won't have children. Doesn't want children, doesn't want heirs. But I'd have children even if they weren't heirs, like the Dersinghams. Hereward says that they think they can lay their ghosts by ignoring them, but you can't. Dead or alive. He says abstinence is the only way."'

'What did you say?' Theodora murmured.

'I didn't know what to say. I wasn't sure I understood her. I wasn't sure I believed her.'

'Do you believe her now?'

Mrs Totteridge looked across at her husband. 'If she meant there are — or were — offspring of the Dersinghams, how could she have known?'

Theodora looked at Alan Totteridge.

'No,' he said firmly. 'We are a family of solicitors and have been since we fell on evil times early in the nineteenth century. Our reputation for discretion is quite unblemished. I've never told anyone about that meeting of my uncle and the Old Baron and I'm sure Uncle Martin wouldn't have either.'

'It's only an inference of yours that the change of will and your Uncle Martin's chance remark mean a child, an heir,' said Mrs Totteridge.

'But quite possible, taken with Amy's remarks,' Theodora pursued. 'Could she have learned from Dersingham or Vanessa?'

Alan Totteridge spread his hands. 'I suppose either is possible.'

'Richard Treadwell,' Theodora offered, 'said that Dersingham had spent a fortune on tracing descendants to find an heir and if there was an heir and the old Baron knew of it, wouldn't Dersingham have known of it?'

'Not necessarily,' Alan said. 'Dersingham was never in his father's confidence and if the heir was a son of his elder brother Leopold, that would have left Louis out in the cold.'

'Would that matter to Dersingham if he hasn't produced an heir himself by now? Might he not just want an heir regardless?' Theodora remembered her conversation with Laura on this very point.

'But if he didn't feel like that . . . ?' Veronica left the alternative in the air.

'And if Amy knew something, is it a fair guess that she got it from Hereward?' Theodora went on.

'And if Hereward suspected that Dersingham might have an heir, why did Dersingham give Hereward the living?' said Veronica.

The thought was in all their minds. 'To keep him quiet?' said Theodora at last and caught the complicity in her host's and hostess's eyes.

CHAPTER TWELVE: CHURCH, LAW AND MEDICINE

'He certainly can't go burrowing about the fabric like that,' said the Diocesan surveyor testily. He spoke of Hereward as though he were still alive, and he made him sound, thought Theodora, like a mole. He might not need a faculty but he'd certainly need an Archdeacon's certificate,' he went on.

'What's the difference?' asked Theodora. It wasn't germane but she was curious.

'About fifty pounds,' said the surveyor succinctly. 'Or, put it another way, if you need more than a hammer or a Black and Decker, it's a faculty job.' He spread the ground plan of St Benet Oldfield church on the desk and smoothed it out. 'The heating system,' he began, and the thick finger traced along the blurred blue lines of the drawing, 'was put in in 1879, originally for a wood-burning boiler to heat water. The old boiler was there.' The finger with its square-cut fingernail stopped. 'That we took out in '47 and put in a coke-fired one and moved it to there.' He stubbed again. 'Converted to oil in '77.'

The surveyor raised his eye from the plan and looked challengingly at Theodora as though he might catch her out in inattentiveness. 'I often think it's a bit of social history, the changes in heating systems in our parish churches,' he said, daring her to contradict.

Theodora, whose admiration for expertise in any area was perfectly genuine, hastened to agree. Indeed, her heart warmed to a man who knew and loved his job. It made a pleasant change after this morning's experience so far. She'd arrived at the diocesan office in the cathedral close at nine-thirty. Not a soul had stirred. She'd stood for ten minutes in the empty hall faced with two tall doors and a closed guichet on the left marked 'Enquiries'.

After a while, Theodora had tapped on the right-hand door and put her head round it. To the informed eye the social and clerical history of the diocese was laid bare. Strenuous efforts had been made to disguise the original character of the room. The original Georgian proportions of what had been the dining room of the Precentor's lodgings had been destroyed in the original conversion of the 1930s by matchboard partitions with frosted glass at eye level. The Precentor had thankfully escaped to a small, warm modern flat behind the choir school. The war had boarded up the chimney and converted the fire to gas. The Festival of Britain had added strip lighting. The sixties had provided plastic and tubular office furniture of an inexpensive kind. The two recesses either side of the fire had seen the addition of a photocopier in the late seventies and a fax machine in the eighties. And there things had rested. The photocopier had an 'OUT OF ORDER' notice on it, and the fax machine was not plugged in. All was silent as the grave.

Theodora had retreated to the hall, knocked more loudly on the other door and walked through. At the far end of the room was a table on which were two typewriters back to back. Facing each other over the machines were, on the left, a small pale-faced girl who looked no more than twelve and, on the right opposite her, a large dark-haired woman with an elaborate dressing of coiled hair.

'It's got the back pay in it,' said the dark-haired one, tapping the envelope invitingly. 'How's your mother?'

'Thank God. I've got a vet's bill for a hundred and fifty. She's terrible. How's yours?'

'Don't know. I had to take Angus up the N and N Monday. I haven't had a minute since.'

'All right, is he?'

'Oh it's fine. Just tests. And his eye of course.'

'Of course. How's . . . ?'

Theodora had had enough of this. She had cleared her throat. Two profiles, the dark and the fair, turned to her. Neither showed any expression which could be called welcoming or, to be just, unwelcoming.

'Diocesan surveyor?' Theodora had murmured.

'First floor, Social Responsibility, second floor, Board of Finance, third floor, Parsonages, fourth floor, Surveyors,' the little fair profile had gabbled rapidly and then swung back to her companion as though loath to be parted.

And so it had proved. At the top of the tight winding staircase, tucked into a beautiful attic room with light slanting in from a northern casement and a stunning view over the close and Tombland, she had found Mr F. H. Heyhoe.

'The pipes,' Mr Heyhoe went on, 'run here and here.' He stubbed with his finger.

'Would Father Marr have known what he was doing, if he started to repair the system?'

'Shouldn't think so. Most of 'em don't know which way's up, never mind something fairly technical like this.' He tapped the lines representing the hot-water pipes put in in 1879.

Theodora recognised the traditional attitude of diocesan servants to their clerical masters: give power to the incompetent and the result is contempt.

'What was wrong with his system?'

'Without going and looking, I really wouldn't know.'

Theodora tried again. 'So what would have to be wrong with the system to make it reasonable to dig a pit just here?' Theodora stubbed with her finger.

Heyhoe reflected for a moment. 'It is puzzling,' he said finally, 'because actually there aren't any bits of the system which run under there. The only thing he's going to hit, if he keeps on digging, is the Dersingham family vault's back entrance.'

'Where's the front entrance?'

'Here,' Heyhoe stubbed the Dersingham chapel.

'Sealed?'

'1951.'

'Ah,' said Theodora. 'I see.' And she did. At last things were beginning to fall into place. She descended the narrow staircase to the empty hall. Through the open office door she heard the two profiles.

'How's the diverticulitis?'

'I can keep it under by walking. Karen's blood pressure's gone up though. And after all that dieting.'

'I've heard Hugh's got shingles. He's in agony.'

* * *

In July 1369, Henry de Spenser, Bishop of Norwich had, with his own hands, hanged rebels from the peasants' revolt from the walls of Norwich castle. In the same year, in a small cell off King's Street to the east of the castle, beside the river Wensum, the Lady Julian, from the Sisters at Carrow Abbey, had lived as an anchoress and meditated on the wounds of Christ, or, as a modern theologian would put it, the problem of evil, the problem of why, in a world held to be created by an omnipotent and benevolent deity, there should be anyone in trouble, sorrow, need, sickness or any other adversity.

As she climbed the steep mound to the castle entrance, Theodora meditated on the contrast: Bishop Henry and Lady Julian, power and prayer. In her darker moments Theodora had reflected on the fact that as a Sister of a house subject to the Bishop, Julian would probably have had to kneel before Henry to ask his permission to take up her reclusive life.

The mound on which the castle stood was an artificial construct thrown up by Norman engineering and Saxon labour, now not quite tamed (it was dauntingly steep) by genteel municipal gardening. Theodora had happy memories of the castle in her childhood as offering the quintessential experience of museum visiting. It was always empty. Or, if there did happen to be stray visitors, they moved quietly, spoke in whispers, avoided the eyes and persons of others upon whom they might happen. They would slide like ghosts around the dimly-lit and echoing galleries where lay displayed row upon row of flint arrow heads, fragments of Roman glass and the none-too-rich gleanings of Danish burial boats. She recalled with particular affection a series of cases illustrating the flora and fauna of the Norfolk countryside through the seasons. They were full of stuffed foxes and taxidermists' robins disposed amongst dried bracken, with painted backdrops of blue skies or grey water. Labels, in faded copperplate, rendered in greenish-black ink, piously attributed the objects to donors with famous Norfolk names: Walpoles, Gurneys, Dersinghams. These were fertile fields in which the young imagination could wander at large. The proper response was left, as in a good liturgy, to the affections of the beholder. Provincial museums, in Theodora's opinion, were not unlike churches: they induced a proper sense of humility in the face of time past, they redressed perspectives and afforded space for stillness and reflection.

Theodora strode eagerly towards the entrance of the museum. The hall was full of people, a disproportionate number of whom seemed to be children too young to appreciate anything properly. Many were eating. Her heart sank. She pushed her way through the milling rabble to the centre of the ground floor, originally the keep which had been roofed over. The castle had lacked windows other than arrow slits when first built but now spotlights and strip lights played down into the central area. There was a plethora of light wood pretending to be plastic. Many objects appeared to be made of fibre glass. Reconstituted materials and reconstructed objects abounded. There was much audio-visual tin-cannery. Gone were the peaceful rows of flints and glass-eyed foxes. There was a slight smell of frying fish and coffee.

Theodora fled like a ghost amongst such uncongenial modernity. Things were utterly changed.

Theodora had come desiring repose, a place to order her thoughts and fit pieces of a jigsaw together before embarking on her lunch with Spruce and Laura. She had supposed that on a fine August day the cathedral might be too full of tourists for that exercise and so had hit on the castle. Now she regretted her choice. She reflected that modern museum display clearly required not passive contemplation of real objects, but busy engagement with pseudo ones, as though the real past was too threatening to be offered to the unequipped public. To appreciate the past you had to be still and attentive but here heritage had driven out history just as elsewhere environment was displacing landscape. The result was as frenetic as a children's playground, where only the noisiest and shallowest responses could find a place.

In dismay she turned to the staircase and with relief beheld the familiar door marked 'Norwich School'. She plunged gratefully into the calm of the art gallery. Half an hour with the Cromes and the Cotmans should be restorative enough. Even here, however, the chatty hosts could not leave well alone. 'Special Summer Event Norfolk Heritage Exhibition: The City at War 1939–45', she read. She turned the corner to find herself confronted with a set of blown-up photographs of the city being bombed. There were black-and-whites of aircraft lined up at Lakenheath with their American crews smiling wholesome, juvenile smiles. There were sepias of girls with padded shoulders and hair curled at the ends serving meals to the soldiery. Gas masks and ration books lay on trestle tables which might themselves have served in the conflict. At the end of the display boards, before the exit door, were a collection of cuttings and photographs taken from the *Eastern Evening News* of the time. Under the title, 'The War on the Land', landgirls in jumpers and breeches were shown looking out from beneath and lodged on top of tractors or at the heads of embarrassed-looking horses. Italian prisoners-of-war leaned sheepishly on hoes. Theodora bent to look at a group of the latter. 'Corporals Bertolucci, Verschotti and Securo at work on the Dersingham estate, May 1944'. Theodora looked again. Corporal Securo, in baggy sepia fatigues, smiled his wide satyr smile from beneath his small neat side cap. In spite of the moustache, there was a distinct resemblance.

* * *

'The Church and the law,' said Dr Maingay, raising her glass, drinking deeply of Charles Julian's Médoc and smiling fondly across the dining table at Theodora.

'And medicine,' said Spruce courteously.

And it was true, Theodora reflected. They were representatives of those pillars of society. Seated formally round the Julian table, in this agreeable, friendly house, the window open on to the herbaceous borders of a late summer garden, how, she wondered, would we look to an observer? Like friends lunching for pleasure? But, of course, they weren't that: they were working men and women, professionals, colleagues, each with his or her own brand of knowledge to contribute. And they were considering why a priest had had his neck broken and been thrown into a pit of his own digging: and what he did to his wife before that and where that wife was now. But, she reflected, it did little harm to conduct matters in as pleasurable a manner as possible. Theodora glanced at her two guests. Spruce, she supposed, must be about forty. He had thick grey hair and very dark eyebrows and eyes. The contrast in colour between hair and eyes seemed to emphasise his vitality. He looked fit, alert, like a Jack Russell terrier. Laura, her spare figure culminating in a long head topped with a mop of brindle hair, resembled a lurcher. And how, Theodora wondered, shall we acquit ourselves, ministers and stewards, over the next couple of hours? Would they have the confidence in each other, in their respective systems, to trust each other, to solve the problem? Certainly she felt that her own perspective might be the one most difficult to communicate. On the other hand Laura had described Spruce as intelligent and humane. He would try to understand. And on such a recommendation Theodora had decided, she was prepared to hold nothing back. Progress would only be made if they shared their knowledge, whatever Gilbert might say.

The wild ducks had gone down well — Mrs Yaxlee knew about ducks. Theodora offered Brie and Wensleydale. Refilling the glasses, she slipped a file from underneath Tobias who had come to roost on the sideboard. 'Hereward,' she said, and glanced experimentally at Spruce and Laura. 'I think we should start with Hereward and Amy'.

Spruce nodded.

'Let us suppose that his killing was not random but intended. Let us suppose, too, that we get, if you like, the murderer we deserve.'

Laura nodded emphatically.

'What he was, who he was, then become questions relevant to discovering who killed him and why.'

Theodora took them through the information she had gleaned from Topstock and from her knowledge of the Society of St Sylvester. 'When we try and get a picture of Marr's own psychology, I think we need to remember the murderous father. It seems to me possible that Hereward may have thought of himself as ineradicably stained by his father's murder of his mother and for this reason he may have felt that he should not himself have children. I think this is borne out if we look at what he wrote in his article on the sacrament of penance for the St Sylvester's Quarterly. What we need to remember here,' she conceded to her secular audience, 'is the nature of sacrament.'

Laura turned her intelligent canine head in Theodora's direction. Next to her particular brand of medicine, what she relished most was theology. Scotland had been rich in theologians.

'Theologians,' Theodora began, 'call sacraments those aspects of our wordly experience which, if used rightly, can lead us into God's presence. Eating, drinking and bathing as well as sexual activity are aspects of our experience which many religions beside Christianity teach us can change our natures and prepare us for ultimate bliss.'

Theodora looked at Spruce, wondering if he was out of his depth. But though his eye rested on his glass, his ears, she could see, were open.

'If we then turn to Hereward,' Theodora took up the article of print from her file, 'this is what he wrote about sacrament and penance. "We need these aids to perfection because we are fallen, imperfect, stained; to use the technical term of theologians — 'sinful'. This state of sin, Christianity teaches, is partly inherited: that is, we are born into a world which is dangerous and corrupting, which feeds us with falseness, brutality and shallowness. But since we can choose, as free agents, which way to turn, whether to wallow in our sin or to repent, the church has devised methods to help us. The traditional form of that help (and we as St Sylvester's priests have, have we not, pertinaciously adhered to the traditional forms) is in terms of confession, which involves admitting one's need, penitence which will seek to make reparation, and absolution which grants a new start."'

Theodora paused to give space for Spruce and Laura to take all this in. She was fairly confident of Laura, but was poor Spruce still with her?

'Are you suggesting that Hereward was trying to live a penitential life because of his father's murderousness?' said Laura with interest.

'His final sentence,' said Theodora by way of answer, 'runs: "in our modern world, the world, after all, in which we are called to exercise our ministry, we have failed to make use sufficiently of this sacrament of penance. Thus we have left our flocks without hope, without any way out of, or back from, their damned state. Perhaps we have neglected this gift of Holy Church by failing to set the example and use it in our own lives."'

There was a second digestive pause.

'What form did this penitence take in Hereward's own life, would you say?' said Spruce with more interest than Theodora felt she had a right to expect from someone who was not, after all, an Anglican theologian.

'This becomes clearer,' Theodora resumed 'as he goes on.' She took up the article again. 'He goes on a bit about fruitful and non-fruitful penance, reparations which do and don't work — quite an interesting distinction that. He certainly wasn't a stupid man. Then he had a couple of sentences about sexual relationships which run: "The root of fallenness is in the female. She tempts. Man is guilty because he gives in to the temptation. But she is the prime source of guilt because she tempts. The only way of righting that relationship is for the woman to cease to tempt and the man to abstain." Then he quotes a bit of Pope Leo, a fifth-century theologian,' she said helpfully, 'who forbade married men entering the ministry to divorce their wives but enjoined continence within it. He was living at a time when there was a debate about whether priests had to be celibate.'

'It sounds idiotic as a basis for marriage,' Spruce said with distaste. 'Why on earth did he marry?'

'If my theory is right,' Theodora answered, 'he has to marry in order to live out the penitential life which his father's murderousness entails on him. Or at any rate to avoid any further perpetuation of the strain.'

'Is there a motive there for murder?' asked Spruce.

'There's a motive for frustration either way,' said Laura.

'There's an excuse, too, for looking elsewhere on Amy's part, if he condemned her to a life of celibacy.'

'A motive both for adultery and the attendant guilt,' said Laura.

'She did want children, according to the Totteridges,' said Theodora.

'It's perverted,' said Spruce almost angrily.

'It would certainly make for tensions,' said Theodora, 'but, after all, is it any stranger than many other aspects of the religious life? Living as brother and sister in a marriage is perhaps no stranger than living walled up in a cell to meditate on the problem of evil. Second-century Christians and the Cathars are said to have done the former, Julian of Norwich did the latter in the fifteenth century. Homosexuality is counted as strange at some periods of history and, in others, quite natural. Is celibacy a deviation? I think we're not quite sure. Chastity would be considered an oddity in some circles and not in others. Many things which we might think are odd can be made to work; things we consider natural might not. It all depends on the spirit in which they are undertaken.'

Spruce had produced his notebook from his pocket and was making notes. He looked up. 'I hope,' he said apologetically, 'you'll forgive my making notes. Your kind hospitality might make me forget the details I need.'

Theodora smiled and filled the glasses. She felt it was a measure of Spruce's quality that he appeared to take what she had said seriously.

Spruce went on. 'What you've told us gives us a picture of someone who might well himself be capable of violence. Was he? Did Amy accuse him?'

'Not to me, but I wasn't specially in her confidence, nor was I present at all the sessions which she took part in at Betterhouse. She might have confided in Gilbert. Indeed his behaviour suggests it.'

'How?'

Theodora considered. She glanced at Spruce. She had resolved to trust him. Only by sharing knowledge would they progress, she repeated to herself. Laura trusted him and so would she. 'He was eager to prevent her returning to Hereward and he was worried enough about her to ring me and more or less instruct me to return her to him if I found her,' Theodora said, and then elaborated on Gilbert's phone call on Sunday.

Spruce started writing in his notebook, taking her revelations about Gilbert in his stride. He'd been right, he felt, to suppose she knew more than she would reveal in the presence of her superiors. What more, he wondered, would follow? 'When did she leave Betterhouse?' he enquired to give her a chance to offer more information.

'She left about a week before I came down here.'

'Did you form the impression when she left that she was intending to return here?'

'I didn't know where she was going. I didn't know where her husband's parish was exactly, though I think Gilbert did say something about East Anglia.'

Laura broke in, 'The local intelligence is that Amy had been away since the early part of June and I've heard no one mention that they knew when she was expected back.'

'So where did she go,' Spruce pursued, 'for the week between leaving you at Betterhouse and appearing here on the Friday of the murder?'

Theodora shook her head, 'As I say, Gilbert might know.'

'I've tried to get hold of Mr Racy via his . . .' Spruce hesitated.

'Locum,' supplied Theodora helpfully.

'Yes. Said he'd left no address for the holiday. I've asked the Met to send a man round to Betterhouse to see if we can prise a bit more information out of them but I've had no comeback yet. When he rang you on Sunday, was he ringing from Betterhouse, do you suppose?'

'I assumed so but, of course, I've no proof.'

'Wherever he was ringing from, though,' Spruce continued, 'he evidently and genuinely didn't know where Amy was, but it does show that she was alive after the car was dumped in the Broad. But what I'd like to know as well,' Spruce went on, 'is where Amy came from. Why did she marry Hereward Marr in the first place and why did she stay with him?'

Theodora reached into her folder and produced the fat envelope with the Italian stamp. 'I think the only piece of luck I've had in this matter so far is in this.'

Laura looked at the envelope. 'Rosalind?' she said.

Theodora nodded. 'The Julians are staying in Tuscany with Reggie Hardnut who was dean here, two back. He's been retired about ten years and he and Audrey bought a cottage there,' she explained to Spruce. 'I got this letter from Rosalind this morning.' She handed it to Laura. 'I expect you know Rosalind's handwriting better than I do. Would you care to give us the relevant bits?'

Laura scanned the letter and read. 'And on Sunday we were asked out to lunch by some old friends of the Hardnuts, Lucio and Honora de Sutto. The oddest thing. They live in one of those places buried in the hills near a village called Pancole (really stunning little church, if you ever are in this area) which looks like a ruin on the outside and in fact is rather luxurious when you get in. We were all milling around before lunch in their nice cool drawing room and there, on the side table, was a photograph of Hereward and Amy, stuck on the end of a group of people I didn't know. Quite extraordinary. To travel a thousand miles to see a photograph of one's own parish priest. As you know, dear Theo, I have no shame and plenty of curiosity. I'm only a bit hampered by my Italian which, you'll be glad to know, is improving by leaps and bounds. It turns out that these people, the de Suttos, were lawyers in Monte Regia where Hereward had his second cure (after Malta, I think it was). There was quite an English colony there owing to Britoil. I gather de Sutto made himself useful to the Brits helping them to buy and sell their properties and he got to know a number of them quite well. Hence the picture, taken at the moment when Britoil finally packed it in. He said he'd known Amy who had been a nurse with the company. In her twenties she'd been rather pretty in a fey way (that fits doesn't it?). Her unmarried name was Foster. She had a mother who lived off her. The father was dead, had been army but not pukka. Anyway, Hereward ten years ago was, apparently, quite good-looking (in his forties, would he have been?) and he and the fey nurse made a match and were married by Reggie in Hereward's own front room. But, I've kept the best bit to the last, the best man was Dersingham! He knew Amy's father. He'd had him in his platoon when he was in the army. He took a liking to Amy and that's why, when Hereward was looking for a living after Warnford's didn't work out, he offered them St Benet Oldfield. So that's one gap filled in. I'd often wondered why and how. I suppose loneliness, perhaps on both parts, and security on hers. We are drinking the local white Vernaccia which is most agreeable. Charles sends his . . . And so on,' Laura concluded.

'What would Mrs J mean by "not pukka" for Amy's father?' asked Spruce meticulously.

'In Rosalind's terms it would probably mean her father was an NCO or a ranker, not an officer,' said Laura crisply.

'What would that mean in marital terms?'

'Given that Hereward's own family were army and pukka, it would mean she started some way behind,' said Theodora.

'Would that be an additional reason for strain?' Spruce enquired.

Theodora nodded. 'I think it's quite clear that Amy's marriage was unhappy and if unconsummated she might have considered it invalid. That would explain why she left the wedding ring in the Dersingham chapel, as a visible sign of her ending it.'

'When did she do that, do you think?' Laura enquired.

Theodora glanced at Spruce. 'What do you have to tell us, Inspector, about the movements on Friday night?'

Spruce pushed his chair further under the table and looked round at them, much as he had done at the meeting at the Bishop's.

'My theory,' he began cautiously, 'is that Hereward might have been killed by someone who wanted to protect Amy. Someone who knew she was being ill-used, or anyway, if your theory is right' — he glanced at Theodora — 'strangely treated and who finally felt she could not stand it or they could not stand it any longer. Into that category, as far as is known to us, comes Father Racy and perhaps Dersingham.'

'You've discounted Amy being the killer then?' said Laura with interest.

'It's not a total impossibility. Presumably nursing experience might give her the knowledge. But it wouldn't give her the temperament. It's just that all I've heard of her so far suggests someone not capable of the anger necessary to break someone's neck so cleanly. In fact,' Spruce turned to Theodora, 'would I be right in thinking, Miss Braithwaite, you agree with me.'

Theodora nodded, relieved that Rosalind's letter with its information about Amy's nursing background confirmed what she had learned from Mrs Totteridge. She hadn't needed to vouchsafe the information herself.

'And,' said Laura professionally, 'she was short of stature. The killer would have found it much easier if he were taller than Hereward.'

'I've already been told,' Spruce grinned at Theodora, 'by Miss Tilley, to probe the movements of every tall person in the village on Friday night. Miss Tilley says she saw a tall figure entering the Rectory at about 11.30 p.m.'

Laura and Theodora watched Spruce as he swirled his wine in his glass. Then he looked squarely at Theodora. 'Does Father Racy drive?'

'Yes, an old Vauxhall.'

'It's just possible,' said Spruce slowly, 'that Racy was here on Friday. Is he a tall man?'

'Not really,' said Theodora loftily, 'he's about my height.'

Spruce smiled, Laura smiled.

'Six foot one or two?' said Spruce respectfully.

'Something like that.'

'Would you mind if, for the purposes of the investigation, I called that tall?'

'As you wish,' said Theodora with dignity.

'Does Father Racy normally wear a cassock?'

'More often than not,' Theodora admitted.

'So you think Racy entered the Rectory after 11.30 p.m.?'

'It's a possibility.'

'Why did he go to see Hereward?' asked Laura.

'Miss Braithwaite's evidence suggests that the marriage was unhappy, that Amy had appealed to Gilbert Racy, that Racy was concerned about Amy's health and perhaps her safety. Perhaps he arranged to meet her here or perhaps he wanted to talk to Hereward.'

'Are you suggesting that Gilbert then killed Hereward in a quarrel about Amy?' said Theodora stiffly.

'I don't think we can rule anything out at this stage,' said Spruce, a clear note of caution in his voice. 'But Hereward was definitely killed at the church and we don't have any evidence that Racy went there, at the moment.'

Theodora nodded, mollified but seeds of doubt about Gilbert began to germinate uncomfortably in her mind. Why had he not told her that he had been at the Rectory on Friday night? His lack of openness, his refusal to trust her at the same time as his wanting to involve her in finding Amy (or was it Amy's box he'd wanted found?) was almost manipulative. But surely he couldn't have *killed* Marr. That was ridiculous.

'When Racy left, would he have taken Amy with him?' asked Laura.

'It depends if Racy was telling the truth about Amy's phone call to him when he telephoned Miss Braithwaite on Sunday. He said that she rang him on Saturday evening. If he is telling the truth, then if she went with him he must have left her somewhere later and when he wanted to contact her again, found she was gone.'

'Or else,' said Theodora bitterly, 'he's disingenuous and he rang me to find out the latest news.' While confident that Gilbert was no murderer, Theodora was beginning deeply to distrust him. There was too much he had not told her.

'Only one thing gives me pause,' said Spruce, 'and that is why didn't Racy get in touch with the police when he learned of Hereward's death?'

Theodora reflected how very tactful Spruce was about not enquiring why she had not revealed everything Gilbert had said to her at their meeting with the Archdeacon and the Bishop on Monday. Perhaps, she felt guiltily, I could have saved him — saved us all — time if I'd had the courage to speak out then. On the other hand it would now be quite impossible to explain to Spruce what someone like Father Racy thought about all non-clerical systems, not just the police.

'I think it would simply never occur to Gilbert to contact the police in the case of any of his clients,' said Laura helpfully. 'He'd regard Amy as his patient, which she is, and as in his pastoral care, which she also is.'

Theodora nodded, grateful for the help. 'He's a doctor — a psychiatrist — as well as a priest. If he thought she needed help, he'd certainly see to it himself. In that, at least, you may be right about his coming down here.'

Spruce nodded. He'd met many reasons for non-cooperation with the police in his professional life. He neatly docketed this in his orderly mind as a new one to take account of if he should ever have to deal with the clergy again.

'Why did Amy return here on Saturday?' said Laura to Spruce. 'Just in order to crash her car into the Broad?'

'Well, it all comes back to where she was when Hereward was murdered and where she went after that. Either she stayed at the Rectory or she went somewhere else for the night, with or without Racy.'

'Are we sure it was she who put the car in the Broad?' asked Theodora.

'We aren't sure of anything much,' said Spruce bitterly. 'Least of all why, if it were she, she should wait until Saturday p.m. to ditch her car or why she went to the Rectory just before that.'

'What about if she left her wedding ring in the church on Saturday, not Friday night?' suggested Theodora. 'If she did that, she might choose to approach the church by the path from the Rectory on Saturday lunchtime because that's a more secluded way of getting there. Then it would be easiest to drive round past the House rather than use the main road, which would involve driving through the village and having to park outside the church which would attract a lot of attention. If she then felt that she'd ended her marriage she might have gone on to make an attempt at suicide?'

Spruce nodded. 'She could have been attempting to take her own life. But it would seem unlikely given there were no keys in the ignition. And I have to say, she chose the least sensible place for suicide. The Broad's very shallow just there.'

Privately, Theodora thought that that was perfectly in line with what she knew of Amy. 'Then,' she said, 'there's the question of Dersingham's wet trousers.'

Spruce looked baffled.

'When the Archdeacon and I went to the Rectory after we'd been to see the Dersinghams on Saturday evening, there was a trail of water across the Rectory floor and ten minutes earlier we had seen Dersingham with dripping trousers.' Theodora stopped. She realised rather late that this was something else which neither she nor presumably the Archdeacon had mentioned to Spruce at the Bishop's meeting.

Spruce looked miffed. 'We didn't get round to searching the Rectory till Sunday afternoon. We weren't sure till after Dr Maingay's post-mortem on Sunday morning that we had a murder on our hands. After all, he could have slipped into his pit and broken his neck. I wish to heaven he had, actually. However, what about Dersingham's wet trousers, in your opinion.'

'I don't know. Could he have met Amy before she crashed the car, or did he go and try to get her out after she'd done so?' Theodora looked across at Laura. 'Is it time you told us about Dersingham?'

Dr Maingay smiled companionably at Theodora. 'I have one or two facts about Dersingham or rather the Dersinghams which may provide us with motives for murder.' She drew out from her capacious handbag a leather notebook and some older looking papers.

'The Dersinghams have, as you know, been here for some years — about five hundred, indeed, in one form or another. Dersingham's father, the old Baron, was my father's patient from 1934 to '47 when he died. I have been through my father's case notes.' She looked down her long nose.

'Old Dersingham first went to my father in June 1936. He was diagnosed as having tertiary syphilis.'

Spruce looked up. 'When would he have had primary syphilis?'

'Approximately ten years earlier.'

'But,' said Theodora, 'the children?'

'Baron Louis was impotent from the onset. It is highly unlikely that either of the boys was an heir of his body. It is just possible that Leopold was. In my view, it is impossible that Louis could be.'

Theodora let out a sigh.

'You will recall that Lady Dersingham was drowned while boating in St Benet Broad in 1937. The family being who it was and the times being as they were, there was no enquiry other than a coroner's verdict of misadventure and there was no scandal. Only sympathy for the bereaved husband and children.'

'Are you suggesting she killed herself?' Spruce asked.

'By all accounts,' said Laura with satisfaction, 'she was a strong minded woman in excellent health. Remember she must have deliberately gone out to get herself a mate to produce certainly one and possibly two sons, that is heirs. Not the actions of a finicky neurotic.'

'You're suggesting she was killed?' said Theodora. 'By whom?'

'It would depend on how keen you were that your wife should be a brood mare for someone else. If you were a normal husband, might you not have felt anger? If you were a husband with a five hundred-year-old name, what might you have felt? He wasn't well, after all. We didn't,' Laura said professionally, 'really get hold of syphilis until after the war.'

There was a long silence. Finally Theodora said, 'Are you suggesting that someone knew all this beside your father?'

'My father's case notes,' Laura said smugly, 'were, of course confidential.'

'I think Vanessa Dersingham may know,' said Theodora after a moment. 'She's embroidering the Dersingham's arms in a lozenge rather than a shield and without the crest. Having done a little research, I believe that would indicate to the heraldically literate that the inheritance went through the female rather than the male line.'

'But what's the connection with Hereward's murder,' Spruce demanded impatiently.

'If she knew that her brother was not a true Dersingham and had no right to the title, might not someone else know?' said Theodora. 'I mean, think about the pit which Hereward dug in the church.'

'The central heating repair,' said Laura. Spruce groaned. He was beginning to hate the pit.

'Well, that's just it,' said Theodora. 'The Diocesan surveyor says it would have no connection with the heating system dug where Hereward dug it. On the other hand, if he kept going, he'd have ended up in the Dersingham family vault.'

'The last member of the family to be buried there being Lady Dersingham, the wife of the old Baron,' said Laura, seeing clearly where all this was leading. 'You think Hereward knew about the possible murder of Lady Dersingham and expected to find evidence of that in the vault? It's been done before.'

Theodora struggled to fit it all together. 'If Hereward had learned about the murder of Lady Dersingham and intended to prove this, and if Dersingham knew what his intentions were, might he not repeat his father's action and kill anyone who threatened his position?'

'And what about his wet trousers?' Spruce said again. 'His statement says he went to Norwich early on Saturday afternoon. He says he came back about four. There's no corroboration for that. He might have been passing the Broad when Amy's car went in.'

'If he thought that Hereward knew about his family's secret, he may have thought that Amy knew too. He may have gone in to find out if she was really dead,' said Laura.

'And is she, by now?' Spruce asked.

'I don't know,' Theodora admitted, thinking of Gilbert Racy.

'Either way,' said Laura, 'it all points to Dersingham.'

CHAPTER THIRTEEN: GEORGE

George stared round the kitchen. It looked much as usual. It was a space cleared in patches for living in but with substantial areas still uninhabited. Like the House, George thought. He put the tray on the table and found his hand was trembling. He'd been shaken by the sounds coming from the study. His dad had always said it was no business of theirs what the family did in private. The tensions, the shouting and anger, the crying in the night, the hatreds, they weren't their business. George, reared from birth not to take too much to heart, to live for the day, the half-day, the fishing hour, was usually able to act on his father's advice. But he found all this upsetting, found it less and less easy to ignore — the unhappiness around him which in some mysterious way brought back memories of his father's death and then, though he could scarcely remember it, his mother's. Things had all been disturbed, somehow. 'That's nice,' his grandma had said of Leon's button. 'Where did you get that then?' Leon had smiled his wide satyr smile and said, 'It is an heirloom.' He'd said the word with pride. He'd looked it up, perhaps in preparation.

'You mean you got it from your dad?' Mrs Yaxlee had enquired.

'My mother. It was a ring but the setting was not strong. It broke. She kept, however, the button.'

'Where'd she get it then?'

Leon looked sideways, 'She told me from my father who got it from his father.'

Mrs Yaxlee had peered at the button, putting on her glasses the better so to do. She handed it back to Leon without further comment.

'Is it a Dersingham button,' George had asked.

'Yes,' she had said tersely. 'That's one of ours all right. One that went astray by the look of it.' She fixed Leon with a wary eye.

'I think, perhaps, I will show it to Miss Vanessa one of these days. After I have given her her riding lesson, would that not be a suitable occasion? She will be interested, yes?'

'Yes,' George had said dubiously. 'I expect that'll interest her.'

Mrs Yaxlee had continued to say nothing. Soon afterwards, the boys had taken their leave.

'Did your ma really give you that button?' George had asked as they edged their way down the path and through the narrow gate of Mrs Yaxlee's cottage. He enquired not because he doubted his friend's veracity, but to prompt him to more if he would.

'Yes. She valued it greatly. She tells me it is part of us. Not just a jewel.'

That had been on Monday. George didn't know if his friend had actually shown the button to Miss Dersingham. He'd been down to the stable on Tuesday evening as he often did, but he couldn't find Leon. Instead he'd groomed Wellington and helped Henry with the feeds, the two of them working well together. George, Yaxlee acknowledged, was quiet, dependable, strong and good-tempered with all the animals. He saw that, and saw too how the boy wanted to be given a job. But what George could not know or guess was how Henry was placed. He could not give George a job without the boy leaving his place with the Dersinghams and without the boy going against his grandmother's wishes. The Dersinghams were Henry's landlords for most of his grazing and, though they never paid the livery bills for their own horses, they were, nevertheless, the name, the local family. As George and he laboured together, Henry reflected on his own plans for his business, so thwarted by Lord Louis. Would these be helped if he enticed his sole remaining manservant from his household?

Henry had bade George goodnight with regret and some guilt. That was Tuesday. Now, on Wednesday morning, George wondered why he felt so uneasy. He'd wakened early and gone in to get the two breakfast trays ready. He'd tidied up the kitchen and done last night's washing-up. Then he would go upstairs to see to Dersingham's clothes. His Lordship's valeting requirements were primitive. He would leave his last night's clothes in his dressing-room. George then went in before seven-thirty and looked them over, cleaned the boots, brushed the jacket and trousers, saw there was a clean shirt and socks, gathered whatever wanted washing into a linen bag and brought it downstairs for Mrs Marge Yaxlee to take when she came in to prepare lunch.

Sometimes, as he busied himself about these tasks, it occurred to George to wonder what his Lordship did with his time. Insofar as the estate was managed, he did, he supposed, manage it. He'd not had an agent for ten years. He spent a lot of time worrying about the fencing and gates and made frequent trips out, often with a hammer and nails to repair, in person, places where the defences had been breached. Though, in spite of that, the cattle seemed to wander pretty freely. He made occasional rare trips to the city, rarer now since he'd retired from the bench. He spent a lot of time in the library. If George had been asked what Dersingham essentially was doing, he might have answered 'waiting'. For in some indefinable way that did seem to George what Dersingham was doing. For what, he could not have said. For death, it had occurred to him to think at times. George did not quite put it to himself that Dersingham's was not a life that should be propped up, but that was what he felt at the moment. What had they ever done? What satisfactions had he had, when had he last, if ever, visibly enjoyed anything?

This morning there'd been a row. Dersingham had a fine talent for manufacturing immense anger quite unexpectedly over apparently trivial matters. This time it was a key. What had George done with it? Which key, George had enquired. You know very well which key, his lordship had suddenly roared. It turned out to be a car key he said he'd had in his trouser pocket on Sunday morning. George had said he'd put the contents of the pocket on the kitchen mantelpiece.

What had he done with the trousers? He'd put them on the creel. Why hadn't he put them back in the dressing-room? They hadn't been quite dry. You had to dampen to press and, in fact, now he came to think of it, they had been damp before pressing. No, they hadn't been, Dersingham had told him forcefully. George had not argued. He sometimes thought that Dersingham so passionately believed his own version of reality that it would have precipitated madness to disabuse him. If he wanted to inhabit his own world, he had the means, just, to enforce that world on others.

Where were the trousers now? Dersingham had gone relentlessly on. George had pointed to the wardrobe in the dressing-room. He'd seen them there on Monday morning. Well, where was the key then? Exasperation seized George. He felt like a misused dog. He simply didn't see what he was supposed to have done wrong. 'Everything in the pockets I put on the mantelshelf,' he'd replied. To which his lordship had responded that he was a bloody deceitful little liar and he was to get him that key now, did he understand? George hadn't understood. He'd retreated, resentful and baffled. He couldn't remember what he'd taken from his lordship's pocket on Sunday, after lunch. He remembered the trousers had been damp. He remembered doing what he always did, emptying the pockets and putting the bits and pieces on the mantelshelf. He remembered pressing the trousers and putting them on a hanger on the creel. He'd not been too interested in what he was doing so he couldn't remember if he'd replaced the contents in the pocket or not. He seemed to remember a dark wet paisley handkerchief, some nails, a bit of twine, three 50p pieces. Had there also been a key mixed up with that lot? There might have been.

George went over to the mantelshelf. There was nothing on it now. He wondered how much time and how much worry he ought to spend on this one. Dersingham was unpredictable. He could make a terrible fuss about something one day and then forget about it completely the next. On the other hand he might go on shouting. George, calm by temperament, found it difficult to cope with shouting. And how had the trousers got back to the dressing-room wardrobe? He was certain he'd left them on the creel. He recalled his Aunty Marge had said Dersingham had come looking for them on Sunday evening. She seemed to think he hadn't found them, so who had, and who had taken them and put them back in the wardrobe. Perhaps they had taken the key? George reflected that if Dersingham hadn't sleep-walked, the only person who could have known where to put Dersingham's clothes was Miss Vanessa. Had she taken the car key? He knew she didn't like Louis driving. Perhaps she objected to him having another car? Taking the key was the kind of mad, highhanded thing she'd do. And, from the sounds he'd heard coming from the library over the last twenty minutes, brother and sister were certainly sorting something out between them.

He went to the door which separated the kitchen from the hall passage. The morning light flooded in from the low windows along the corridor, making the wide, sand-scoured floorboards look white. George found himself tip-toeing as he moved along the corridor to the baize door which opened on to the front hall. Carefully he opened the door and listened. All seemed quiet now. He heard someone coughing in the library — the door, he saw, was not quite shut. He remembered how as a child he had moved around the house on, as it were, a track of sound. In those days, all of ten years ago, the staff had run to three or four servants beside his father, who was reckoned an outdoor servant, but who had constantly been in and out of the house as he did his repairs to keep the fabric and the artefacts more or less functioning. His father had remarked that he had seen the House shut down, first wing by wing, then room by room until only the six rooms of the central block remained in use. So George had moved round the House steering himself unobtrusively from coughs to hoover, from door closures and door openings, to floorboard creaks to tray clatterings; the golden rule, not to be seen or heard. Now, to his experienced eye and ear, it felt as if the way was clear. It seemed he might be able to gratify Leon's curiosity.

'Please George, my friend,' Leon had said, 'I am so very much wanting to see it. It is a fine House, a castello, yes?'

'No,' George had said firmly. 'It was never fortified. It's not a bit like a castle.' He was quite sure of his idea of a castle since he'd visited Norwich many a time and admired the great castle walls, even enjoyed the museum part.

'Well then, it is still a very fine House. Please let me look at it.'

Reluctantly, George had agreed. It did not seem an odd request to George, just a difficult one to gratify. In a similar position George himself would have wanted to see the local sights and the house was certainly that. Miss Vanessa was easy to avoid. She kept to her room till lunch most mornings. His lordship generally went out on Wednesday morning to mend his fences so George reckoned that, between about half-ten and eleven, he could show Leon the main rooms.

As he hovered in the doorway, George tried to remember what his father and grandmother had told him about the history of the house. He knew anecdotes attached to some of the artefacts: the playing cards the Prince of Wales had used, the fat one, not the present one; the nicknames of some of the portraits and the names of the horses on which earlier Dersinghams had been depicted. But he found it hard to put these scraps into any kind of context: he had no history of public events to which to fit these domestic details. But he did have a feeling for the solid presence of the House: its proportions and furnishings, the casements and door locks, the shutters and fenders; for fabric rather than colour, for shape and balance rather than style or taste, for objects, in fact, as they had to be cleaned or mended. He knew what he would show Leon. Things, to his mind, were 'well-made', rather than 'beautiful' or 'eighteenth century'. But there was little that he did not know by eye, touch and smell. He inhabited the House quite as much, sometimes rather more, than those two upstairs.

George listened once again, carefully. After a minute he heard the cough leave the library and make its way, tap-tapping up the uncarpeted main staircase. He withdrew his head from the door and went back to the kitchen. Leon stood, framed in the back doorway.

'It is convenient?'

'He's out. She's just gone up to her room. A clear run.'

They set off at a long-rein walk, not unlike a couple of ponies. George was fair-haired and heavy, Leon small-boned and reddish-brown, the two striding forward in accord. George began to enjoy his task, entertained by Leon's nimble cavorting as he took up the rear. They progressed from the library, dining room and study on the ground floor and mounted the stairs to the first floor. The glory of the wide gallery opened before them and George was pointing out an example of the banisters of the gallery which his father had repaired so well that you couldn't tell the difference, when they heard the shot. Unhesitating, George bounded up the last two steps and gained the door at the end of the gallery. Miss Dersingham's room was square and high ceilinged. On the floor, between the bed and the desk, lay the figure of Lord Dersingham. The sun caught the glint in his hand of a revolver so small it looked like a toy. Near his head was Miss Dersingham's tapestry of her family arms, cut and gashed to shreds.

CHAPTER FOURTEEN: ST SYLVESTER

'This is Father Lucy,' said the voice.

Theodora felt she remembered it from somewhere. She could not now recall where. 'Good evening,' she said briskly, tapping her pencil on the top of Tobias's complaisant head as he sat beside the phone in the Julians' drawing room. 'I'm afraid Bishop Julian is away at the moment. Theodora Braithwaite here. Can I help you?'

'It's you, isn't it?'

Theodora forbore to make the obvious reply. It was an irritating voice, she thought.

'Didn't you ring to know where Gilbert was . . . is?' it asked.

Of course, Muriel's stand-in from Betterhouse. 'Oh yes, of course, yes, I did. How kind of you to ring back.'

'Yes, well. He's at the Sisters from tomorrow.'

'The Sisters?'

The voice lost all patience. 'We have a sister house at East Soken over near Diss in Norfolk. Where are you?' the voice added, in case she had lost her orientation. 'Father Gilbert rang to say he'd be there Thursday for the celebration. If you still want to talk to him, that is.'

'Yes,' said Theodora, suddenly alert. 'And where is he now?'

'That, I am very much afraid, I can't reveal.'

Doesn't know, thought Theodora. 'I'm very much obliged to you for taking so much trouble.' She wondered whether she should add she hoped they might meet some time. No. Better stick to the truth.

'That's all right,' said the voice of a very young man suddenly disarmed.

Theodora put the phone down. After Spruce had been called away from the luncheon party, she and Laura had sat in companionable silence, by common consent putting aside the problems of Church and state. At four, Spruce had rung personally to tell her of Dersingham's death and asked her to come up to the House. The next few hours had been hectic. The Bishop had rung, the Archdeacon had rung. The first seemed inclined to blame her personally for Dersingham's death, the second had suggested what indeed Theodora had already prepared herself to do, that she should go to Miss Dersingham.

At the House, she had found a subdued but competent George and his aunt making tea for large numbers of the constabulary. George had shown her up to Louis Dersingham's room, since the police would not let Miss Dersingham use her own. He had tapped on the door and then left her. There was no response to the knock, but Theodora had entered nevertheless. She found Miss Dersingham seated at the window. Theodora drew up a chair and took her place opposite her. Theodora knew there was nothing one could do for those who suffer except sit beside them: anything else is impertinence. So she sat. Miss Dersingham in no way acknowledged her presence. She did not cry but from time to time swallowed convulsively. After an hour, Theodora had risen to go. Miss Dersingham had stretched out her hand to retain her and for a while they had sat, the old woman and the young linked together. Towards the end of their time together, Miss Dersingham had spoken, not much but to the point.

It had been late evening by the time Theodora had returned to the Julians' to field the telephone call from Father Lucy. But in the light of all that had happened, she knew now what she could do. She reached for the previous week's copy of the *Church Times* on which Tobias was sitting.

There it was, on the second to back page: 'The Society of St Sylvester will hold its festal high mass and annual reunion at the House of the Sisters of St Sylvester, East Soken, Diss, Norfolk, on Thursday 29 August. Mass 11.30 a.m. Concelebration. The senior of the Society, Canon Gervaise Stringer, will preside. Preacher, the Bishop of Sevenoaks. Those wishing to concelebrate please notify Father Topstock at the House by Monday 20 August. Accommodation overnight available at £4 incl. breakfast. Luncheon after Mass, please notify Sister Superior.' That's it, she thought. Gilbert will know at least some of the answers; the best thing to do is to go and net him amongst the fathers of SS.

* * *

The house of the Sisters of St Sylvester had been difficult to find. The good weather, which had held up until now, had been replaced by heavy dark clouds which swept low across the sky bringing first lightning then thunder and a torrent of rain which settled, after a while, into a heavy, thudding downpour. Peering through labouring windscreen wipers, Theodora had sought in vain for signposts. These had given out after Diss. She had driven down cart tracks, followed scarcely comprehensible native Norfolk directions to 'go cross the drain' and finally, about to abandon hope, had found, deeply buried in a hedge, the familiar arms of St Sylvester painted in dark green on a light green board, the equivalent, Theodora felt, of washed-out green biro. She had bumped up the rutted drive and stopped in front of a substantial square white Victorian country house. A circle of single storeyed brown brick cells sprouted from one end and terminated in a windmill, the sails and roof of which had been replaced with a shallow glass dome surmounted by a gilded cross.

As if to make up for the paucity of directions in the surrounding countryside, the community had provided a wealth of instructions. A knee-level signpost with five arms offered chapel, oratory, guest house, refectory and office. Theodora took the last at its word. At the front door the same eager plethora of information met her. 'If open, push, if closed, ring,' said the handwritten notice in faded ink but vigorous with flourishes. Inside the hall, ranged against the near wall, were a pile of assorted sized and very clean Wellington boots placed side by side as though awaiting feet. The notice here said, 'Wellington boots, please scrape off mud.'

The heavy silence of the place, contrasting with the battering of wind, rain and windscreen wipers over the last hour, brought Theodora to a halt. She stood and snuffed the familiar air of a religious community. Every object, every surface was preternaturally clean. Brass vases glowed, the hall table glittered, the stair-rods shone, the immense life-size wooden crucifix on the wall opposite the front door had been oiled and polished. The floor looked treacherous as ice. In the corner by the stairs, the long case clock beamed its loud tick into the quiet hall. It said ten o'clock. As its large hand reached the hour, a bell tolled out near at hand, and a moment later soft sounds of scurrying feet, like moths, came from the corridor. Theodora, schooled in the ways of communities, waited and was rewarded, after a moment, by a very small nun springing at a fast gallop across the polished floor. She kept her footing on the slippery surface with admirable dexterity and slid to a halt in front of Theodora.

'Miss Braithwaite? You are most welcome on our festal day. You're almost our first guest. I think you said on the phone you would like a word with Sister Superior? She's still in the oratory but if you'd like to come and wait in the parlour, she'll be free in a little while. I forgot, did you say you'd be with us for lunch?'

Theodora recognised the voice for what it was, that of a person needing to respond to a number of different requirements, not always compatible with each other; the need to get and give a large amount of information in a short time fought with the requirement to be very quiet about it. 'If that doesn't make the numbers difficult,' Theodora answered, copying the nun's soft tone.

'On our festal day, all are welcome. Of course you can lunch. That will make seventy-six,' the nun concluded in a triumphant whisper as though she were beating some personal best. 'If you would care to come this way.'

She wore the pre-Vatican two-black-veil-and-grey habit, the only concession to modernity being, as far as Theodora could see, that the habit was perhaps half an inch shorter than it might have been when the sister had entered the novitiate. The nun bounded agilely off and Theodora strode after her. It was impossible to tell the age of her escort, although, despite her sprightliness, she was clearly not a young woman. No hair showed, no make-up had been used for years and the result was that, though the lines of goodwill were deeply etched in the round, chubby face, she could have been anything from forty to seventy. Theodora was struck, as she had been before, by the fact that there never appeared to be any obviously middle-aged nuns. They were either girls or old, spry women.

'How many are you in the community at the moment?' Theodora made conversation.

'An apostolic twelve,' said the agile nun with pride as they wound their way down miles of polished corridor. Theodora found it possible to orientate herself by the way in which the smell of boiling greens approached or retreated as, presumably, they swerved around the pole of the kitchen. She wondered if she had been wise to agree to lunch. But it seemed unlikely that, after her late arrival, she would have time to ask all she needed to ask of the Sister Superior before the Mass and it might well be that she would have to stay on until the guests had gone.

The fast-moving nun stopped at last in front of a door marked 'parlour'. She flung open the door and allowed Theodora to pass in before her.

'Is Father Racy here yet?' Theodora enquired on an impulse.

'I'll tell Sister you're here,' the nun said, and sprinted off, leaving Theodora gazing after her. Had she heard, was she deaf, did she not understand or was she not going to tell? she wondered. The room she found herself in was bleak. An engraving of the founder, the Reverend Henry Thomas Newcome, hung over the empty fireplace. There were a great many copies of the St Sylvester Quarterly Review in the bookshelves and two uninviting upright chairs. Theodora looked at her watch. A quarter past ten. The silence had descended again. She paced up and down trying to quieten her impatience. She wanted Gilbert, she wanted the Sister Superior. The next time she looked at her watch it was half-past. She went to the window.

In the rain-swept drive below her, a number of cars were beginning to arrive. From out of them tumbled priests of all shapes and sizes. There were bent and grizzled old priests, one at least pushed a Zimmer athletically before him, refusing the support of two nimble youngster priests. There were hale-looking middle-aged ones and thin ones with the yellow pallor which suggested a life in the mission field of the east. All had narrow clerical collars and were dressed in clerical black suits. Many carried small attaché cases containing doubtless their cassock, albs and stoles. In the swirling rain Theodora could hear fragments of greetings tossed about on the wind. Jeromes and Gervaises, Geoffreys and Gregorys, Christophers, Michaels and Timothys were gathering in their clan.

Large clerical umbrellas shot up with the crack of artillery fire. Theodora drummed her fingers on the sill. What on earth was she doing up here? Where was the Sister Superior? Why had she been deposited here, far away from the action? The thought flitted across her mind that she was being deliberately kept apart from the gathering.

She returned again to gaze down from her high perch. Now a few laymen with the odd wife could be seen dodging the puddles. They were not, for the most part, young, but they looked, for the most part, prosperous. A minibus with 'St Botoph's United Catholic Youth' painted by hand on its side, drew up in a cloud of spray, and eight strong-looking youths dressed for a day's rock-climbing in coloured anoraks debouched onto the wet gravel. Theodora decided the time had come to descend. It seemed Sister Soup wasn't able to get away. Indeed she would need to be greeting her guests by now. Her best plan was to mingle and see if she couldn't find Gilbert and arrange to see him after Mass.

She went to the door and attempted to open it. The door did not respond to the handle being turned, indeed the door knob went round and round making no contact with the retaining flange. A wave of irritation swept over her. Why should these gentle, hospitable sisters lock her up? She could not believe that she was deliberately being imprisoned. Surely it was just that the catch was faulty. On the other hand, she wouldn't put it past Gilbert to engineer such an outrage. He certainly had influence here. Theodora looked closely at the fitting. It was secured to the door with two perfectly ordinary screws. She reached into her handbag and took out her clasp knife with the screwdriver attachment. The wood was old and poor quality pine. The screws came out easily, the knob detached itself from the spindle and fell into her palm. Then she pushed the spindle through and heard it fall onto the floor in the corridor outside. Finally, she inserted the end of the screwdriver attachment into the hole left by the spindle; it caught on the edge each side and turned nicely in her hand to release the tongue of metal. Theodora strode purposefully down the corridor in the direction of the noise.

The journey back was not as easy as the journey up had been. The corridors all looked alike. Some had fire buckets in them, some not. No other distinguishing mark was apparent. Hastening now, impatient to bring matters to a climax, she turned a corner and came up against a door marked 'Fire Exit'. Impatiently she pushed at it. It resisted for a moment and then flew open. A blast of rain-laden wind drove her back into the corridor. She closed the door and turned round. At the end of the corridor a tall figure was turning the corner. Theodora hesitated. 'Gilbert!' she called, her voice echoing through the silence of the building. The figure swished its cloak and was gone. Again Theodora felt anger rise within her. She was beginning to find Gilbert's evasions melodramatic and tiresome. She began to run down the empty, uncarpeted corridor. She sped round the corner. A cul-de-sac of three doors confronted her. She tried the one in front of her. It was locked. She tried the right-hand one. It contained shelves stacked with furniture polish. In exasperation, she flung open the third. She found herself peering into a large empty room, lit only from the central dome. In the middle of the room, directly beneath the dome, was a small table, beside which sat a cassocked figure of great age, its hands folded over a stick. It sat so still Theodora wondered if it were a statue. She sought its eyes which were located under low-lying eyebrows. They were closed.

Theodora framed her question but hadn't the nerve to utter it. She was on the point of retreating when the eyes snapped open. The priest raised a hand in a gesture like the God of Michelangelo's Sistine Chapel. Then, leaning slightly forward, in the deity's pose, towards his own outstretched finger, the figure intoned in a high ecclesiastical voice, 'That is the way.' Theodora backed out. She retraced her steps to the fire door, forced her way out into the teeth of the wind and driving rain, turned left and then right and found herself outside the front door.

Father Topstock's substantial figure and bald head were stationed in the porch. Courteously, he held open the door for her. 'How nice to see you and how kind of you to come and support us on our festal day,' he said cheerfully. 'Staying for lunch, are you?'

The ordinariness of the meeting after the nightmare of the last ten minutes overwhelmed her. 'Thank you, yes, I hope to,' she said distractedly. 'Have you seen Father Racy, by any chance?'

'Over at the back, I think, by the stairs.' Topstock gestured vaguely into the hall which was now packed with wet and drying clergy. They were stacking coats, discarding, could it be, yes, it was (where did they buy them nowadays?) galoshes. They twirled dripping umbrellas and filled the large hall with as great a degree of noise as there had previously been depth of silence. Far away to the right, Theodora caught a glimpse of purple. Sevenoaks had arrived then.

Theodora's height helped her as she surveyed the black crowd, searching for Gilbert Racy or the Sister Superior. There were one or two ancient nuns easing the more decrepit of the priests from their black gabardines, but there was no way of knowing whether any of them was the Sister Superior since all the sisters would be eager to play the role of hospitable handmaids on an occasion of this kind. Of Gilbert she could see no sign. She began to move round the room, edging her way from group to group, catching snatches of conversation.

'I had two very good days on guilt,' she overheard a young dark priest say to an older fair one. 'Sin, of course, I could not mention, but I can't manage without guilt.' She squeezed her way past them and skirted a tight knot of closely integrated priests of about the same age discussing parameters, networking, learning curves and gender issues.

She had almost reached the staircase when the bell began to toll. The priestly crowd, with no abatement of noise, turned towards the front door and began to troop out, heads down, into the driving wind and rain, towards the truncated, cross-surmounted windmill. Caught up in the movement, Theodora was swept along, still anxiously scanning the gathering. She found herself pacing beside a short, springy young priest with a healthy tan. He smiled at her briefly. 'There won't be many of your sort here, but' — he dropped his voice and leaned towards her conspiratorially — 'actually I'm all in favour. I think the Bishop of London was right. The work of deacons is best done by women. I work in Southwark,' he added by way of explanation.

'So do I,' said Theodora. She heard the tension of the last half-hour in her voice but she forced herself to be comradely. 'St Sylvester's Betterhouse.'

'Ah. Gilbert's here. I think he's concelebrating. We shall doubtless see. Are you staying for lunch?'

Theodora nodded, quickening at the mention of Gilbert. They entered the chapel together, genuflected and made for the low benches on the north side, like birds of a feather. Suspended high up on the wall opposite the altar, Theodora glimpsed a box containing the choir of four men and four boys, recognisably the United Catholic Youth. The rows were filling up. Dark grey light from the glass-domed roof high above filtered down the long brick cone of the mill chapel onto the mass of black bodies. The wind shouted outside and the rain rattled on the glass.

Within the building, silence deepened. The two candle flames on the altar guttered in the occasional draught. Twelve concelebrating priests sat, six on either side of the altar, their heads uniformly sunk into their shoulders, eyes veiled or closed. Behind them, in a second row, Theodora counted the thirteen sisters of the community, eyes, like those of the priests in front of them, turned inwards, their hands decorously hidden in their habits. Nothing would disturb that double rank of praying men and women now. The Bishop was seated to the north of the altar, his silver curls peeping out from either side of the mitre and clustering on his angelic profile, the light blue cope falling in perfect folds to the floor. He looked just like a Firbank bishop, Theodora thought, her self-possession returning to her through the silence. But she reflected, she had heard the Bishop preach and knew he was no ninny. Opposite him, on the south side of the altar, on two chairs, Theodora recognised the old priest whom she had disturbed under the dome fifteen minutes ago, presumably the Senior of the Society, the Reverend Canon Gervaise Stringer. Next to him was Gilbert Racy. Theodora relaxed — so her journey had not been in vain. She gave herself up to the ancient drama about to be unfolded.

Into the deep silence came a single note from an unaccompanied counter tenor, 'Kyrie, eleison'. The voice was true, confident and full of promise. We are in good hands, thought Theodora with gratitude.

All knew their parts to perfection. There was no fumbling. Incense and music rose and fell. Altar boys came and went. Hats and mitres were punctiliously put on and taken off. The gospel was sung, bells tinkled, the elements were consecrated, the host held aloft. Together they prayed the collect of St Sylvester that 'we may in such wise order our affections inwardly and our conduct outwardly that having fulfilled all duties both public and private, we may not at the last fear to come to thee who liveth and reigneth . . .' As befitted a Bishop of Rome who became confessor to the first Christian Roman Emperor, St Sylvester hit, Theodora thought, a nice balance between religion and politics.

There was much, of course, she admitted to herself as the liturgy swept on, that was mere flummery and boys-gamishness. But nevertheless, she was, as always, moved by the concentrated, unified power generated by the exactly executed ritual. Ritual, she reflected, was after all a way of rendering our deepest inner experience in dramatic terms. It was the common language of the inner life translated into the aesthetics of light and dark, sound and silence, movement and stillness. They were praying now for the recently dead of the society and those laymen who were its prominent supporters. 'For the souls of thy servants,' Theodora heard, 'Hereward Marr, Louis Dersingham.' There was a crash which Theodora took at first to be the thunder of the storm, then, with a rush of alarm, part of the building collapsing. But, almost immediately, she realised that one of the nuns ranged behind the priests on either side of the altar had slid to the floor, overturning her chair. In a flash Theodora remembered. There were thirteen nuns ranged behind the priests. One too many. She rose to her feet and slipped swiftly down the aisle to the back of the chapel. This time she had no intention of being evaded. She flung herself through the swing door to the outside world, turned to the right and raced round the circular wall of the mill to the place where the altar must be inside, the liturgical east end. Sure enough, there was a small vestry built onto the chapel and connected by a covered walkway to the low brick cells. Two nuns were supporting a cloaked figure down the walkway.

'Amy!' said Theodora sharply. The nuns hesitated for a moment and the thin, colourless face turned towards her.

CHAPTER FIFTEEN: UNHAPPY ENDINGS

'What about the hens?' Theodora said severely.

'I got someone to feed them,' Amy said defensively. 'Are they all right?'

They were sipping their sweet Indian tea in the community's very clean sitting-room. The supporting sisters had left to see to their guests. Gilbert would be down in a minute, they explained, when he'd divested and seen to the Bishop.

Bishops, thought Theodora, are like very young children. They need to be escorted everywhere, called for, taken back, helped with their coats and their galoshes, fed and watered at regular intervals and exposed only to such company which was suitable for them. Theodora was glad Gilbert was having to nanny a Bishop. She felt an ill-defined anger towards him. She felt he had played games. Hide and seek was no activity for men in their fifties.

'So when were you at Oldfield and when did you leave?' Theodora asked Amy as the latter huddled on the large, uncomfortable sofa.

'Gilbert came for me on Friday, last Friday.'

'After you came down the Julians' drive?'

'Yes.'

'Why did you visit the Julians'?'

'It was you. I thought . . . I mean I hoped to see you. You'd said you were going to Norfolk.'

Had she? How very careless of her. She'd know better in future. 'Why,' said Theodora mystified, 'didn't you stop, then?'

Amy started sobbing. 'I lost my nerve, I . . . You looked so tall and composed. I just felt I couldn't.'

Well, really, Theodora thought crossly, if she was going to be hampered in her pastoral work by her height as well as her sex she might as well give up.

'Where,' she enquired testily, 'did you go next?'

'I said. I went to the Rectory.'

'And?'

'Gilbert picked me up from there.'

'Look, Amy,' Theodora said in exasperation, 'Hereward is dead. Someone killed him. Did you?'

'No,' Amy said sullenly and added, 'And Gilbert didn't either.'

Theodora nodded. Amy's tone dispelled any doubt Theodora might have had. She'd not really believed Amy had it in her physically to destroy anything.

'The police will need to know a lot more about your movements and actions from Friday night to Saturday afternoon. I really think it would save us all a lot of time and emotion if you told me what you know.' She restrained herself from adding that it would also give the woman some practice in telling the truth in a coherent manner. Amy looked deeply into her tea mug. 'Could I have some tea?' she said appealingly.

Theodora swung the huge tea-pot over the mug and then waited forcefully.

'I take sugar,' Amy said.

They're so manipulative, fumed Theodora, aware that she was failing to show the patience she should. She thrust the basin in Amy's direction.

'Well,' Amy began, 'after I left you in the Julians' drive on Friday I went to' — she hesitated — 'I went to the Rectory.'

'Did you go straight to the Rectory?'

'If I'm going to tell you, you've got to let me tell it in my own way. Gilbert says it's important to let it flow.'

Damn, damn, damn Gilbert, Theodora thought, not for the first time. 'I'm sorry. Please go on,' she said, forcing herself to be gracious.

'There were no lights on but I knew Hereward was in. He used to walk about in the dark, you know. He said it was his natural element.' Amy stopped. She seemed to have lost her thread. Then she gathered herself together again. 'I found him in the end. He was in the library mixed up with his books. He'd been drinking. I don't know where he gets the cash. We quarrelled, of course,' she went on tiredly. 'Why was I never there? Why had I gone away? Why had I come back? How long did I think I was staying? I mean it's all so pointless. It doesn't really matter whether I'm there or not. He only notices me when he wants something to torment. He finished up with his usual ploy about "didn't I realise what it was to be the wife of a priest?" I just laughed at him. You know, I wasn't his wife. Not really.'

'I know,' said Theodora gently. After all, she told herself guiltily, the woman had truly suffered.

'You know?' asked Amy startled. 'How?'

'I read his article on penance in the St Sylvester Quarterly. He touches on his theology of marital relations.'

'Oh yes, that. I don't understand all that theory. I'm more practical. I trained as a nurse, you know. A long time ago.' She seemed scarcely to believe in her own previous career.

'Yes. I know that too,' Theodora assured her. 'I gather you were good at it.'

'Good?'

'You nursed Ted Yaxlee in his last illness.'

'Yes, yes, I did. He was a really, really nice man, Ted.' There was warmth and affection in Amy's tone. 'He was clever too, good with his hands, right up to the last, and he was funny. He made me laugh.'

Theodora waited patiently. Amy lifted her eyes to Theodora. 'I suppose you'd better know the lot.'

Theodora nodded.

'Well, as I said, we quarrelled, Hereward and I, as we always did. We were well in, when Dersingham barged in. Must have been about eleven, I suppose. He had a key to the Rectory and he just walked in. He often did that. I suppose having given Hereward the living he felt he had the right. It used to annoy Hereward more than somewhat. Though in a funny sort of way they were friends too. They'd been at the same prep school and they carried on a sort of rivalry. Always trying to get one up on each other. Absolutely childish. They used to get drunk together and they had the same interest, you know.'

'Genealogy?'

'Yes. That's right. Dersingham was obsessed with trying to find descendants for his name. His precious name.' Amy paused, then said, 'It was an awful shock to hear him prayed for in chapel just now. I didn't know he was dead. He is dead, I suppose?'

'Yes,' said Theodora quietly.

'When?'

'Yesterday morning.'

'How?'

'He shot himself with a horse pistol in his sister's room.'

Amy winced. 'I'm not surprised really,' she said bleakly after a moment. 'Anyone connected with Hereward seems to meet with disaster, or suffering anyway. He couldn't get it right somehow.'

'Friday night,' Theodora prompted.

'Yes. He came in to tell Hereward something. Some discovery he'd made about an heir.'

'What would that have been?'

Amy ignored her. 'Ted Yaxlee was a nice man,' she said inconsequently, 'and Hereward snatched him from me.' Amy began to cry quietly again. 'I'd come here just for the weekend, just to get my breath back. I used to do that, you know, come here. The sisters are very kind and Gilbert used to fix it with them for me. I knew Ted was ill, of course, but I was sure he'd last another week at least. Well, he didn't and there was only Hereward with him at the end. I supposed Hereward weedled it out of him. Or perhaps Ted was just wandering by that time.'

'What did Yaxlee tell Hereward?'

'About the heir. Only he wouldn't have been an heir, only a descendant. But Hereward said Louis didn't care in the end whether it was heir or descendant. He just wanted to find someone of his own blood. I think the nearer he got to his own death the more he wanted someone, anyone. Ted served the Dersinghams all his life and his father before him. There wasn't much they didn't know about the family one way and another. But he never judged them, you know. You never felt with Ted that, however they behaved, he was judging. He was like that with everyone. I never felt guilty with Ted.'

Theodora utterly understood. Poor Amy.

'He told me first. We used to talk about a lot of things when I visited him. He knew from his father, of course, because he was only a boy himself at the time. But his father had known there was a son and Ted said there was a grandson by this time. But it would have been a descendant not an heir. The title can't go through the female line.' Amy sounded as though she might be repeating something Hereward or Dersingham had said. 'Miss Victoria, you know the one killed over fences. Well, during the war there were Italian POWs working on the Dersingham estate and Victoria fell for one of them and had his kid. A boy. Of course they kept it from the old man who was mad as a hatter, apparently, and would have killed them both. Ted said he'd killed his wife but I don't know if that was so or if it was a bit of gossip.'

'What happened to the boy of Victoria's?'

'Ted said she went away to have it and then the father took it back to Italy with him. I think a fair amount of money changed hands by what Ted says.'

'Then what?'

'Well, Victoria was killed off her horse Festival of Britain year. Ted was around by then of course, and he was there when it happened. He and Henry Yaxlee both used to help with the horses. I suppose she killed herself in a sort of way.'

'How do you mean?'

'Just before she went out on that day, Ted told me his father said he handed her a telegram. It was from the Italian lawyers who dealt with the child's father. His name was Leon something or other.'

'Leon what?'

'Sutto, would it be? Or, no, that was the lawyer's name. Victoria's chap was called . . .'

'Securo?' Theodora supplied.

'Right. Well Ted told me, when she'd read the telegram that morning, she gave it back to him, that is to Ted's dad, and said "He's dead." That's the last thing she said. They brought her back on a gate a couple of hours later.'

'Who did Ted's dad think was dead, the father of her child or the son?'

'Ted said his dad wasn't sure. It could have been either. It wasn't clear.'

'The telegram?'

'Ted said his dad was at a loss what to do with it. He thought it might be too important to destroy. So he kept it.'

'And you say,' said Theodora, 'that Ted Yaxlee told all this to Hereward before he died?'

Amy nodded.

'If Hereward knew all this about the telegram and he surmised it was the son who was killed, had he told Dersingham about it?'

'No, not until that Friday night. When Dersingham came in on Friday night they just went on about genealogy. They both ignored me. As I say, it never really mattered whether I was there or not. They just carried on the same.'

'So Hereward and Dersingham discussed the son of Victoria and Leon Securo. Then what?'

'Well, it emerged that Dersingham had found out about Leon Securo, Victoria's chap, from somewhere, he didn't say where. Then he'd gone and traced him up in some war photographs in the *EEN*. He said he was getting his lawyers, Hardnuts, to try and find out what had happened to the Securos. Then Hereward butted in and told him not to bother because though there had been a son of Victoria and Leon, the boy was certainly dead. And when Dersingham asked for the proof, Hereward said' — Amy smiled gleefully — 'that there'd been a telegram the day Victoria died saying so and that telegram had been buried with her.'

'What?' said Theodora incredulously.

'Ted didn't care for Hereward. And he liked a joke. He reckoned he'd give Hereward a bit of a chase. Put him to a bit of trouble. Ted gave me the box with the telegram in it about a month before he died. But I gather from what Hereward said after he'd taken Ted's funeral that Ted must have told him before he died that his dad had made a box for the telegram and put it into Miss V's coffin. She was put in the family vault of course and Ted's dad was a pall-bearer.'

Light dawned on Theodora. 'So Hereward had started unsealing the Dersingham family vault to get at the box.'

'Right.'

'When did he start digging?'

'There wasn't much opportunity until the heating went wrong and then Hereward thought that would be a good excuse. He wanted to taunt Dersingham, I think. Show him he had some power over him. He knew Dersingham was desperate to find someone to take on the estate when he died. Hereward wanted to show him he was doomed to failure. He seized a spade round about Wednesday.'

Time enough for him to dig deep enough to be found dead on Saturday, Theodora reflected, if Dersingham wanted to prevent him getting at the box.

'Where was the box really?'

'As I said, Ted had given it to me before he died. I left it in the Dersingham chapel with my wedding ring when I finished my marriage.'

'And when did you leave the ring there?'

Amy hesitated. She's going to lie again, Theodora thought. Given the omissions she'd made so far she didn't hold out much for Amy's inventions.

'I left it there before Gilbert took me off that night.'

'What time did Gilbert come to the Rectory on Friday night?'

Amy clasped her tea cup in her small hands and avoided Theodora's eye. 'How can I remember? It's all a blur,' she said with actressy passion.

'Amy, were you and Gilbert and Hereward all in the church on Friday night?'

'Yes, no. Oh, I've told you Dersingham and Hereward . . . then Hereward went off to dig and then Gilbert took me away.' Amy started crying again.

'You mean that before you came to the Sisters with Gilbert you made him drop you off at the church and you left the ring there?' Theodora could not keep the incredulity out of her tone.

'Yes,' said Amy sullenly. 'Why shouldn't I have?'

Theodora sighed. 'What about the car?' she began, and saw a nun's head appear at the door behind Amy. She continued urgently 'Amy, you came to the Sisters in Gilbert's car. Well, what about your car? Where did you leave it on Friday night?'

'Father Gilbert asked me to say,' said the sister smilingly, 'he's very sorry but he has to drive the Bishop to the station and then he must go straight back to London. He's so very sorry to miss you both.'

Amy said firmly, 'I can't say anything more without Gilbert. I've told you all I know.'

'Amy are you saying Hereward was killed by Dersingham that Friday night?' Theodora pressed her.

'Dersingham? Well, I expect that would be best, wouldn't it?' said Amy as though confronted by a new but not unwelcome thought. 'Since he's dead after all.'

* * *

'I'm not sorry'. Henry Yaxlee turned to Theodora as to an equal and looked her unflinchingly in the eye. 'I don't regret a thing. Him. He should have been put down long ago. He shouldn't have been born. He should have been stopped. His Church should have stopped him, God knows, doing the things he did.'

'They didn't know,' said Theodora, aware that she too was being judged.

'Why didn't they know? It was their business to know. They're quick enough to gossip. They should have got some facts. They should have taken some care.'

'Yes,' said Theodora penitently, 'we should.'

From outside in the stable yard came the sounds of hooves on paving in a nice, rhythmic walk. The storm had cleared while Theodora had raced across country. The air was fresh with perhaps a hint of salt in it from the estuary. Nothing, however, of the beauty of the countryside had dissipated her anger against Gilbert Racy. Ambiguous as his attitudes and communications had been earlier, his last defection had convinced her that he'd manipulated her throughout this affair. He'd done his very best to stop her finding Amy when he must have known that producing her would have saved everyone — the police, her friends, the Church even — an enormous amount of time and worry. He'd prevaricated and evaded and left her to do the worrying. About finding Hereward's murderer, he'd cared not at all.

Henry's tall figure stood square and upright in the small office. On the table before him was a tangle of sweet smelling stirrup leathers which he'd been saddle-soaping. Had he been calming his nerves, Theodora wondered. Had he known she was coming?

'How did you know it was me?' Henry said. 'I can't believe Amy would tell. She loves me as truly as I love her.'

'No. It was nothing that Amy said. She was, in her way, discreet. Your name was barely mentioned. I think it was the hens. I asked myself who cared enough about hens to shut them up every night. It was you, wasn't it?'

'Oh yes, I saw after them all right. Amy was very attached to those hens. I couldn't let them get taken. There's a vixen comes over from Nether Oldfield coppice most nights to see if I've done the job properly. So I rode over on old Wellington any time I could get away during the day to feed them and shut them up at night. I hoped Dersingham's cattle would cover the hoof prints and I used to go up the bridle path. It isn't much used. It was chancy, but I couldn't let Amy down.'

Theodora remembered the figure on horseback she'd glimpsed from the top of the St Benet tower. Had that been Henry on Wellington dashing out to feed the hens?

'The other thing which made me think you cared about Amy and might feel as you do about Hereward was the phone call.'

'You mean the one on Monday night, when I rang the Rectory?'

Theodora nodded. 'On Monday night I went over to the Rectory to get a book out of Hereward's library. While I was there in the library the phone rang.'

'I was afraid you might have recognised my voice,' Henry said. 'But I had to ring. When Gilbert took Amy off on Friday night, he didn't say where he was taking her. I didn't know where she'd gone. I suspected she might have gone with Racy to London but when I rang the Betterhouse number they said he'd gone on holiday and couldn't be got. I was worried sick because she usually rang me when she was away and she hadn't so I wondered if she'd gone back to the Rectory. It was a chance. I got wondering when the phone was picked up. But Dersingham wanders in and out of there and I thought at first it might be him.'

'He was there,' Theodora admitted. 'He was drunk and asleep amongst Hereward's books.'

'That figures. Drinking and sleeping and shouting. That's about all he's up to. He doesn't have many talents.'

'There are just one or two things I don't quite understand,' Theodora said hesitantly.

Henry nodded as though giving her permission to enquire. He took up a leather and began to chafe it through his strong-looking hands.

'What about the goat's collar?'

'Ah,' Henry smiled with genuine amusement. 'It was that damned box of Ted's with his telegram in. Evidence,' he gave Theodora a warm smile, 'of Miss Victoria's fling. I couldn't think what to do with the thing.'

'Why not just throw it away?'

'That's what I did. I sunk it in the Broad. But, of course, Ted was a wood-carver. The box was a nice piece of box wood and it'd have floated, so I had to weight it. I hadn't any twine on me to put a stone with it, so I took the old goat's collar.'

'You knew George and Leon fished it up?'

'That Italian's lucky isn't he? He's got talent and luck. He'll do better than the rest of the Dersinghams. Did you know he's got a button off the family's livery which came down from his grandad? He's been showing it round. Showed it to Miss Dersingham, Miss Vanessa, that is. Showed it to her the evening before Dersingham killed himself.'

'How many people knew about Miss Victoria's liaison?' said Theodora curiously.

'One or two may have suspected. I don't suppose the Dersinghams were the only ones to fall for the charms of the Italians. But the Dersinghams were pretty close, on the whole, and Ted was loyal. I knew because Amy told me what Ted told her when he was dying.'

'Did Hereward know?'

'Reckon he got it out of Ted too but Ted told him the telegram was hidden in a box buried with Miss Victoria so he . . .'

'Dug up the vault,' Theodora finished. 'Yes I know. I think Dersingham knew too. He'd found pictures of the Securo boy amongst Victoria's things, then he'd looked at the contemporary photographs of the POWs in the *Eastern*

Evening News and finally he'd asked his lawyer to trace the Securos.'

'Had he too? Amy didn't mention that. Poor old Dersingham.' Henry fiddled with the leather. 'Why do you reckon he topped himself?' he brought out suddenly.

Theodora looked at him. She reckoned he had a right to know, all things considered.

'I sat with Miss Dersingham last night,' she said slowly, 'She told me that after Leon showed her his button she'd thought about telling her brother a descendant appeared to have been found. In the end she didn't. The reason she didn't was that she'd recently found some letters. One was addressed to herself and one to Leopold, the eldest son who hanged himself. They were from Lady Dersingham before she died. I gather what they said was that the old Baron was too sick to provide her with sons so she'd found someone else to do so. What I mean is Louis and Leopold weren't Dersinghams. In the end she told Louis just that.'

Henry smiled broadly. 'Best news I've had today,' he said, 'that Dersingham wasn't one.' Given his dislike of the family, Theodora found his delight in finding that Louis didn't belong to it slightly illogical.

'So now there aren't any more proper Dersinghams,' said Theodora reflectively. 'They can't inherit through the women so Leon doesn't count,' Her tone changed. 'Henry,' she went on more briskly, 'that night, Friday night, what happened exactly? Amy's account wasn't too coherent.'

'I'm not surprised,' Henry said warmly, his anger returning in remembering. 'She was distracted, poor duck. Well, she came and saw me after she'd been down to the Julians'. I tried to tell her that it was time she left Hereward and we could start afresh. She said she was that frightened of Hereward, she didn't dare leave him. I said she must and that she must go and tell him so that very night. I offered to come with her and she said, "give me an hour and then come on if I haven't come back".'

'So?'

'I did just that. I saddled up old Wellington and went down the bridle path to the Rectory. There was no sign of either Amy or Hereward. I couldn't think where they'd gone. Dersingham was asleep, drunk, in the library. I went on up to the church. They were both there. We had a row. Amy was sobbing and beside herself and in the end she took off her wedding ring and put it on the finger of the crusading lady. She said something like, "that's the end of my marriage which was never a marriage." And Hereward slapped her face. I went for him and I broke his neck.' Henry was breathing heavily as he recalled the scene.

'I put him in his own pit — his spiritual home, I reckoned — and took Amy back to the house. Racy had come. I told him what I'd done. I expected him to turn me over to the police. But he didn't seem too interested in that. He took Amy in hand and said he'd look after her. I agreed it was best to get her away for a bit. So that's that.' He ended flatly.

Theodora found she was near to tears. 'What about the car? Amy's car?'

'Yes, well, I made a bit of a pig's ear about that. She'd left it here, of course, when she went to the Rectory because she didn't want it known she'd visited Hereward. And it's only ten, fifteen minutes' walk along the bridle path. So I had to think what to do with it. She'd left me the keys so I put it out of the way in the garage overnight. Then I drove it over next morning with the idea of leaving it outside the Rectory. Which I did. I left the keys in it, in case she came back. That afternoon Dersingham returned from Norwich. He didn't know at that time that Hereward had been killed. He just knew Amy wanted to leave him. So when he found the car he thought perhaps Amy'd left. He had some idea that if the car was found in the Broad people would think that Amy had drowned and she could disappear and there'd be no further trouble. You see he didn't think priests ought to get divorced and he certainly wasn't having one of his going through that sort of scandal. It was better everyone thought she was dead. He made a right cock-up as you'd expect. He chose to put it in down by the low pond entrance to the Broad so, of course, he couldn't get it in far enough. I expect he had to climb out and get his feet wet and no one was deceived. I gather the keys weren't in the car when it was pulled up, so I expect they're still in Dersingham's pocket knowing him. Oh, no, of course, he's dead. I keep forgetting.'

He came to an end.

Theodora said gently 'What will you do?'

'I shall survive. I'll do my time and I'll come out and I'll run my business, my stable, again. My past won't destroy me.' Henry wasn't boasting, just stating. 'No right-thinking man here will blame me. That I can tell you.'

'Is there anything I can do?' she asked diffidently, 'To help?'

'You can keep an eye on Amy. She's not strong. And Wellington, too, though I expect George will look to him. My cousin Ben'll run the business while I'm inside. You can always trust your own. Tell Ben to take young George on. He'll be looking for somewhere now and he's a good lad.' He looked impatiently at his watch. 'That Inspector should be here by now.'

There was a sound of a car in the yard and a blue flashing light reflected itself in the glass of the office door.

Henry put his keys on the desk and glanced at Theodora. 'I don't know when I'll be back,' he said firmly. 'So I wonder if you'd do me the kindness of giving my keys to Ben. He'll take over from now on, until I'm back. He'll be up about six to do the feeds.'

Theodora nodded. Henry looked at the Inspector framed in the doorway. 'Right,' they said together, and walked side by side to the waiting car.

EPILOGUE: UNHOLY GHOSTS

The people's warden tolled vigorously. The bell leaped to respond with light high B flat which could be heard in all three villages of Oldfield, Oldfield St Benet and Nether Oldfield. The last induction of a priest to St Benet Oldfield had not turned out well. Whatever the Bishop had found for them this time could not but be better. 'No way to go but up,' Father Topstock, brought in at the last minute to do the music, had murmured to the warden a moment ago as he mounted to the loft to take his seat at the organ five minutes before the service.

The congregation — forty-two, counting the youngest addition to the Yaxlee family, little Sharon (two months and couldn't be left) — rose to its feet. The organ started on Zadok the Priest. The choir, all four of them, two short Yaxlees and two tall ones plus a crucifer, the Archdeacon and the Bishop, processed. The organ modulated to 'Now thank we all our God' and the congregation joined in with what for Norfolkmen was fervour.

The church smelt of chrysanthemums. The congregation could see their breaths before them in the cold October evening air. The central heating was not working. The induction of Thomas Wesley Treadwell, Master of Arts of

Cambridge University (and, as it happened, youngest son of the current Archdeacon of Norwich) as the fifty-fifth incumbent of St Benet Oldfield was under way.

Theodora sat on the second row, south aisle, sandwiched between the tweed-clad figures of Bishop Charles Julian and his wife. In the front row she could see Laura Maingay's cheerful red hat and beside her the neat figure of Inspector Spruce. She glanced across at the Dersingham family chapel at right angles to the altar. It was empty. There were no more Dersinghams. Leon, the only descendant, wanted to return to Italy and the art to which he gave all his intelligence. The one remaining Dersingham, Miss Vanessa, had surprised everyone by retiring to a very small, very modern bungalow at Cromer. The estate, she had indicated, would be sold. The crusading Lord Dersingham and his lady gazed with blank eyes towards the stone roof.

Deaconess Tilley had completed the reading of the second lesson.

'Now thank we all our God, we have just sung. And so we should,' the Bishop was saying. 'So we should thank our creator God for the rich stream of our Anglican tradition which, down the centuries, has irrigated the soil of our common life; for the riches of scholarship and poetry, of music and architecture. But, above all, we ought to thank God for the example which the Church has afforded of godly and righteous living, found, of course, in all faithful Christian people, but especially in her clergy, who, ever open to the prompting of the Holy Ghost, have guarded and sustained their flocks.'

Theodora looked across at Thomas Treadwell, fresh-faced, fair-haired, beardless and newly led to his stall, about to take up his first living. 'God guide, comfort and sustain him in this his ministry,' Theodora prayed silently, for how else will he manage at all?

'Plain sailing,' said the Bishop heartily, 'is not to be expected. Our disabling past haunts us and may at times inhibit our best efforts. Practices, people, places even, can become unholy ghosts impeding for a space, at any rate, the free flow of that true Spirit which seeks continually to realise God's kingdom amongst us. So it is this evening that we must pray that our past may be a source of strength and a cause of hope to us, not an obstacle in our paths or a door which locks us out from fruitful change.'

Theodora thought of Marr and Amy and the Dersinghams, none of whom had made wholesome use of their pasts. She thought of the Church's own attitudes to change, its clergy, so often uncertain or ungenerous, saying the right things but not always doing them.

'I think I can assure you,' the Bishop smiled kindly, directing his gaze on Thomas, 'that in the ministry of this young man, you will be well served. After all,' he chuckled, 'I know his father.'

The congregation smiled with reserve. They'd seen them come, those with fathers, and they'd seen them go. Some of them had come croppers. Who his father was didn't count, the Yaxlees reckoned. Time alone would tell with this one.

THE END

THE JOFFE BOOKS STORY

We began in 2014 when Jasper agreed to publish his mum's much-rejected romance novel and it became a bestseller.

Since then we've grown into the largest independent publisher in the UK. We're extremely proud to publish some of the very best writers in the world, including Joy Ellis, Faith Martin, Caro Ramsay, Helen Forrester, Simon Brett and Robert Goddard. Everyone at Joffe Books loves reading and we never forget that it all begins with the magic of an author telling a story.

We are proud to publish talented first-time authors, as well as established writers whose books we love introducing to a new generation of readers.

We have been shortlisted for Independent Publisher of the Year at the British Book Awards three times, in 2020, 2021 and 2022, and for the Diversity and Inclusivity Award at the Independent Publishing Awards in 2022.

We built this company with your help, and we love to hear from you, so please email us about absolutely anything bookish at: feedback@joffebooks.com

If you want to receive free books every Friday and hear about all our new releases, join our mailing list: www.joffebooks.com/contact

And when you tell your friends about us, just remember: it's pronounced Joffe as in coffee or toffee!

ALSO BY D.M. GREENWOOD

THEODORA BRAITHWAITE MURDER MYSTERIES

Book 1: CLERICAL ERRORS

Book 2: UNHOLY GHOSTS

Printed in Great Britain
by Amazon

46478838R00118